Judgment Reversed

Judgment Reversed

RICARDO D. PALACIOS

MCM Books, July 2020

Published in the United States by MCM Books, Austin, Texas.

ISBN: 978-0-9967473-5-6

Library of Congress Control Number: 2020939810

Colophon

Designed and edited by Alfredo E. Cárdenas.

Frank Saldaña, Esq., performed legal review.

Impact typeface was used for chapter titles and Adobe Caslon Pro typeface was used for the body text.

Dedication

To the memory of our dad

Ricardo Daniel Palacios

November 13, 1943 - December 15, 2018

from his loving children
Ricardo Daniel Palacios Jr., George Abraham Palacios,
Antonio Ignacio Palacios and Virginia Elizabeth Palacios.

Chapter One

Reynaldo García snubbed out the cigarette in the court clerk's crystal ashtray. He noticed the Río Grande Auto Parts logo under the ashes. He blew out a long horizontal column of smoke. The smell of burning paper and tobacco enveloped him. He glanced across the crowded courtroom and noticed his adversaries sitting at a table laughing at something one whispered to the other. He hated waiting for jury verdicts.

He looked at the 1982 calendar on the wall and counted the days to his next trial. He had practiced law in Laredo, Webb County, and South Texas since 1967, and through the years had waited for many jury verdicts. He knew he should be back at the office working, but his clients usually demanded he stay and wait, in case a last minute problem came up. Today was no exception.

Reynaldo walked among the court personnel and opposing counsel. He stood a foot or two taller than most people. While he was considered a tall man in any group, he towered over most Mexican Americans, who were the predominant population in Webb County. His powerful broad shoulders and large thick hands, made him look threatening. Pale Yankees envied his light brown complexion. He wore hexagon lens glasses and a thick straight Chaplin mustache. A thick mane of graying hair topped his head, adding emphasis to his bulging green eyes, thin lips, and broad face. He was handsome, in a rough sort of way, in his neatly pressed navy pinstripe suit. He often quoted a movie cowboy in describing himself, saying a man should be feo, fuerte y formal.

His legal opponent on this occasion was Mario Cantu, a close friend since childhood when they often mixed it up on the school playground. Now, they fought each other in the courtroom, and in legal matters, on an almost daily basis. They were about the same age. Mario was of medium build and was light complected and exhibited a slight paunch pushing out a buttoned vest. His black horned rim glasses matched his thinning black hair and he had to crane his head back to look at his old friend Reynaldo eye-to-eye. His broad flat nose distinguished him from most men. They had both lived in Laredo all their lives, except for the time away at college and law school. They went to the same elementary, grammar, and high school where they were both involved in school politics.

In 1979, Juan Pérez came to Reynaldo with a legal problem. Pérez owned a cattle ranch consisting of 2,200 hundred acres. Ten years before, his sister Minerva Pérez sold her adjoining cattle ranch to a local businessman by the name of Larry Flores. Each had inherited an equal share from their mother who had divided her inheritance between her two children. Later, Pérez noticed Flores ran an advertisement in the newspaper where he had his ranch up for sale and claimed to own 2,400 hundred acres.

Pérez began to scour maps, tax statements, and surveys. He checked his fence lines and the maps more than once and found that one of Minerva's fences stretched three hundred feet too far north, taking in two-hundred acres of his property, acreage Flores now was trying to sell.

Pérez almost cried. Little brought a South Texan to tears, a loss of land, being one of them.

Reynaldo filed a lawsuit on behalf of Pérez against Flores, to recover the 200 hundred acres. Flores hired Cantu to represent him in the lawsuit. The trial lasted six days, and both attorneys were exhausted. At seven o'clock in the evening of the last day, the jury asked for sandwiches and settled in for deliberations on a full belly. Reynaldo had hoped the judge would have refused the request for food, then the jury would have finished and hurried home for supper.

At about nine o'clock Reynaldo strolled into the almost empty courtroom. It was a large square room, paneled in dark wood, with sparse fluorescent lighting set in a dropped wafer ceiling, contrasting with a deep burgundy carpet. About the middle of the square, a three-foot high wooden barrier, the bar, divided the room. On one side were the theater chairs for the public, on the other side was a large elevated wooden bench, and two large counsel tables surrounded by massive captain's chairs. To the right of the judge's bench, at a distance against the wall, was the jury box containing twelve seats for the jury.

Pérez, his wife and their two sons sat in the audience area talking. The scene reminded Reynaldo of a wake, people staying up until the early hours of the morning talking about everything.

The opposing counsels struck up a conversation about politics and current events. Reynaldo and Mario, while opposing counsel, were still friends but no longer as close as when they were kids.

Thirty minutes after nine three loud bangs came from the jury room door, which meant they had reached a verdict.

"We have a verdict!" The bailiff shouted as he hurried through the courtroom to the judge's chambers across the hall.

The attorneys and clients straightened-up and quieted-down. The jury streamed through the courtroom, single file, and took their places in the jury box. At this cue, the rotund judge, draped in a black robe, strolled out of his chambers.

"All rise! The 184th District Court in and for Webb County is now in session, the Honorable Carlos Zapata presiding," the bailiff cried out in a loud trailing voice.

"Ladies and gentlemen of the jury have you reached a verdict?" Judge Zapata asked.

"We have reached a verdict, your Honor," jury foreman Charlie Gonzalez said in a tired voice.

"Bailiff, please get the verdict from Mr. Gonzalez and give it to the district clerk," the judge instructed. The paper made its way across the room, and the fat middle-aged lady with the dishwater blond hair took the paper with her right hand, holding it at a distance as if it offended her. She placed the paper in front of her on the desk next to the judge, adjusted her glasses, then grabbed the paper with both hands, brought it to the front of her face and began to read the questions and answers.

Reynaldo sat next to Pérez at the plaintiff's table, and wrote the answers on the blank verdict form, grinning and hissing, as the clerk read out each of the answers. Pérez nervously sat by, not knowing whether his attorney was reacting in despair or out of pleasure.

After a long monotonous delivery, the young lady finished and plopped down.

"Ladies and gentlemen, is this your verdict?" Judge Zapata asked.

The jurors, one by one, nodded and grumbled yes.

At this Reynaldo stood up, his deep rumbling voice drawing everybody's attention.

"Your Honor, the plaintiff moves for judgment on the verdict."

"Yes, yes, ah, yes, I think so," the Judge agreed. "Judgment is granted for the plaintiff. The plaintiff's attorney will prepare the form of the judgment for the court's signature. Please submit the judgment to Mr. Cantu, allowing him the opportunity of objecting timely, if he so desires."

The judge thanked the jurors and advised them that their check for jury duty would be mailed to them. The attorneys and clerks picked up papers and briefcases. Reynaldo explained the jury verdict to his client, telling him that they had won. He asked him to come to his office the following week to discuss developments, if any. As Reynaldo began walking out, he almost bumped into Mario. They smiled, reached out and shook hands.

"You did a good job, Reynaldo," Mario smiled, "but of course, you know I am going to appeal. I can't let this jury verdict sit, you know that."

"You're dead in the water Mario, why waste time and money taking this thing up on appeal?" Reynaldo asked as he walked out of the courtroom shaking his head, leaving his colleague behind.

Reynaldo stepped through the courthouse door into the hot night air. It smelled of dirt, gasoline, and oil. His leather heels clicked on the concrete sidewalk. He walked to his office and thought of Mario's threat and shook his head.

As he walked, he noticed the dim streetlights reflecting on the cobblestone street. He thought of his early friendship with Mario, the trial, the city, the land, the people, his ancestors, and things and places of long ago. He thought of the stories and histories that his Grandmother Maude had told him, undoubtedly passed down by her father Lorenzo Galvan and his fathers and mothers before him. Reynaldo had heard the stories all his life. He knew his family and community's history, and he reveled in it.

Chapter Two

Spaniards first explored and settled South Texas and the area surrounding present-day Laredo, Texas, in the mid-1700s. The land consisted of vast grassy plains, with rivers and creeks flowing east toward the Gulf of Mexico. The intense weather did not discourage the colonists, as they slowly began to establish rancho after rancho, in return for land from the Spanish Crown.

Among the Spanish settlers were the most eccentric and rambunctious members of wealthy Spanish families, enlisted soldiers, and some peasants. This mix made up a typical South Texas Spanish settlement.

On May 15, 1755, Capitán Don Tomas Sánchez established the village of Laredo on the left bank of the Río Grande River, also known as the Río Bravo. The twelve founding families multiplied to one hundred, as the small village flourished. The settlers farmed acreage close to the river and raised beef and smaller animals, ganado menor, on the vast plains surrounding the pueblo.

Reynaldo remembered Grandma Maude explaining how the settlers constantly fought the elements and the Comanche, Apache, and bandits. And how the homes had rifle and gun slots built into the walls, enabling the inhabitants to shoot out at the aggressors without directly confronting them. She explained the problems with the weather and how the sizzling summer heat would turn to ice and snow in January. Notwithstanding frequent attacks, disease, and the merciless elements, the ranchos

flourished, and the strong became stronger, and the strongest became the trailblazers. Despite lack of military protection, and without help from the central government in Mexico City, they survived. These were the ancestors of most present-day Laredoans, including Reynaldo, an eighth-generation descendant of Don Tomas Sánchez.

As the decades went by things changed in Mexico City, and at points northward, but little changed in Laredo, except the population, which swelled into the thousands. When Mexico declared a war of independence from Spain, Laredoans managed to keep a low profile, and stayed out of the fracas. Some individuals from the township helped one side or the other, but as a whole, the community was uninterested, uninvolved, and unaffected.

With independence from Spain won, Laredo became a part of the Mexican Republic. While they felt they were Spanish or Mexican, Laredoans, most of whom were related by blood, considered themselves an autonomous community.

The most noticeable change after independence was the number of travelers that came through, either from the north on their way to Monterrey or Mexico City, or vice versa. Surprising to most in Laredo, many of the travelers were Anglo Saxons, typically called Anglos. In the meantime, Mexico City encouraged some of these Anglos to settle and colonize the northern part of the Mexican Republic in the state of Coahuila-Tejas.

Rumblings of difficulties among the Anglo settlers and Mexico City were often heard, and Laredoans remembered the difficulties they too experienced with distant authority. They felt more aligned with the Anglos, experiencing similar challenges and problems with their far away government that excised money and cattle at will without compensation or protection.

Before long, the differences between the Anglos and Mexico City were irreconcilable. On isolated trips to San Antonio de Bejar, Laredoans saw armed pioneers and small groups of militia in every settlement. A few Laredoans moved north to San Antonio de Bejar, and when visited by relatives from Laredo, confided that, if pushed, they would fight on the side of the Anglos against Mexico.

Soon Laredoans knew the Anglos, and their Tejano allies, had had enough. Grandma Maude told Reynaldo that one afternoon her grandfather, also named Lorenzo like her father, heard the bugles blaring and drums rolling. Word spread fast, the Mexican army was on its way north. The army chose to cross the river at the Presidio del Río Grande, upriver from Laredo. The whole pomp and strength of the Mexican military rode through the dusty streets of Laredo. Mexican General Antonio López de Santa Anna crossed the river with four thousand soldiers, some mounted but most were infantry, each in their starchy white pants, blue coats, and tall black French hats.

They marched north to quell the Anglo rebels who refused to follow Santa Anna's orders. Despite the many soldiers, rifles and the long cannon and howitzers, the expedition resembled a pleasure trip. They brought along musicians and whores. Grandma Maude told Reynaldo how her father, then a boy, got to hold General Santa Anna's white horse when he dismounted at the Plaza to receive greetings from the community's leaders. The entourage camped out in Laredo for three days, and although a few merchants expected to get good business from the large contingency, they voiced disappointment and displeasure, as the soldiers took what they wanted without paying. The excitement at the sight, sounds and smells of weapons, troops, music, and campfire food, turned to fear as the days passed. Laredoans voiced no disapproval when the army marched north.

The news filtered down about the massacre at San Antonio de Bejar and the last stand at the Mission of San Antonio de Valero called the Alamo. The story of the revenge at the battle of San Jacinto preceded the straggling Mexican soldiers. Grandma Maude's grandfather later explained to her how the soldiers swam across the wide river at Laredo or paid to get skiffed across on a chalan. They rushed through Laredo crossing the river cowed, defeated, and afraid. They were not organized either, it was helter-skelter, to get across. Laredoans hoped the war would leave them alone, untouched and it mostly did.

In 1840, nearly a century after its founding, a small band of Laredoans and others that occupied both sides of the Río Grande, displeased with edicts from Mexico City, declared their independence and formed a sovereign republic of their own, La República del Río Grande.

The settlers established its seat of government at Laredo, the largest house on San Agustín Church Plaza being designated the capital and Jesús Cárdenas as President. They claimed as its geographic area Tamaulipas up to the Nueces River, Coahuila north to the Medina River, Nuevo León, Zacatecas, Durango, Chihuahua, and New Mexico. The self-proclaimed republic lasted less than a year, as opposition and failure to attract support led to its demise.

After the Mexican American War ended in 1848, Laredoans were pleased when they heard that Mexico and the United States of America came to peace after the Mexican American War, but were surprised to learn that under the Treaty of Guadalupe Hidalgo, they were to become Americans and were no longer Mexicans. The new border between the two republics was now the Río Grande, and being on the north bank, they became Texans. Some were displeased and scurried across the river and established the sister township of Nuevo Laredo. Most, however, had learned to live without a national government and were not afraid to be a part of the United States.

With the new political arrangement, however, came a horrible hatred by the Anglos for anybody and anything Mexican. Discrimination and prejudice, which the Spanish Mexican colonists had never experienced, swept the entire state. Trips northward became dangerous, and only traveling in large groups ensured safety. Life in Laredo, however, was mostly unaffected, as no Anglo dared start a racial conflict in a large Mexican community.

As the years passed, the prejudice took hold and gained momentum in Texas. Mexicans or anything Mexican was unwelcome. This, even though many Mexicans or Tejanos fought side-by-side with the Anglos against Santa Anna at the Alamo. Being born in the Republic of Texas, or being Spanish, and not technically Mexican, made no difference to the Anglos.

Laredo developed its own subculture and went on through history unmolested. But the prejudice, bias, and discrimination spread throughout the State of Texas, and beyond its boundaries into the United States. The hatred continued for more than a century and from generation to generation.

Chapter Three

Reynaldo walked through the streets, thinking about the just-concluded trial, and how special land was to Laredoans and to South Texans. He thought about how Grandma Maude explained early Spanish history while they sat in the dark on the porch at her home. She sat on her rocking chair and he on the porch's top step.

He could see with the light coming from inside the house and his abuelita's hair slightly blowing from a cool southeasterly breeze. In the background he heard the sounds of crickets chirping, and an occasional neighbor or horse passing by competing with her voice. To his delight, she sometimes talked until midnight.

She explained that the Spaniard's future depended on manpower and how most of them had large families. Families of ten or twelve were not uncommon. Diseases usually claimed two or three children.

The elder in the family prayed for boys to help with the ranch work. Her family was no exception. Her own father Lorenzo Galvan, great-great-grandson of Capitan Tomas Sánchez, the founding father of Laredo, was one who believed in large families.

His great-grandfather Lorenzo, called Lore for short, was born in 1828. He grew to be a strapping man of medium build. He married one of the Gonzalez girls who gave him twelve children. Five daughters never married, and marauding Apache killed one of his sons. Grandma Maude was the youngest child, and she married Juan Francisco Javier Pérez, and they had several children, including Martha, Reynaldo's mother.

Reynaldo, who was the great-grandson of Lorenzo Galvan, heard the names of the varied family members all his life but did not truly understand the connection until seeing a genealogical chart in 1975. He learned that he descended from the famous Captain Sánchez, and as it turned out, was related to just about everybody in Laredo, including his old friend Mario, his client Juan Pérez, and Judge Zapata.

As the families grew large, the inevitable happened; a few remained wealthy, but most became poor. Most people got to the point they did not even know they were related, and some unintentionally intermarried.

Lorenzo inherited much land and cattle. As a wise business-man, he accumulated much more, and most of his children, in turn, inherited large ranches from him. Even to the third generation beyond him, it was not uncommon for a descendant to at least have a small ranchito of up to five hundred acres.

Laredo's warm climate, its proximity to Monterrey, and its access to railroads helped make it the nation's largest inland commercial port. Its community character of friendliness, diplomacy, independence, and their care for family and culture, resulted in the creation of one of the truest and least known melting pots in the Americas. The Anglo immigrants that came to Laredo were so outnumbered that their only option was to marry into local Spanish speaking families. The Polish, Italian, French, Greek, English, and German found wives in Laredo. Jews also married Mexican Catholics. Grandma Maude explained that different cultural holidays were celebrated, and customs and ideas were exchanged and intertwined into the local Mexican culture, which dominated the others. But all races and religions joined and blended in Laredo. Grandma said this added to the individuality and uniqueness of the community, and its character; and a hospitality that continued to attract many more.

Reynaldo was born in 1943 in Laredo, the product of the marriage of Martha and Adam García from Val Verde County.

Mario's grandfather Louis migrated from Monterrey, Mexico, and grew to love Laredo, his adopted home. His son Louis married Ernestina Gutiérrez of a Spanish pioneer family, and one of their offspring was Mario, born in 1942 in Laredo.

Reynaldo reviewed the family tree with awe. He had not known he was related to most of his classmates, friends, and even to people he disliked. Nor did he know he was a descendant of Capitan Sánchez and Ramon Martin, the rich Frenchman in town.

Laredo became a beautiful place of many cultures, but unfortunately, the rest of the State of Texas, and some other parts of the United States still hated Mexicans and anything and anyone even resembling Mexican. Laredoans who traveled in other parts of the state brought back the distasteful stories of being refused admission, food, or lodging simply because of their Mexican heritage.

In fact, most people in Laredo who grew up isolated and insulated from such discrimination expressed amazement on hearing the stories and only partially believed them. When they traveled north, they experienced the discrimination but strangely, felt unaffected. The bias was against someone else, it could not be against Laredoans, they thought.

Chapter Four

A week after the verdict, Reynaldo and his wife Mari Lou joined his client Juan Pérez and his family for dinner at the Country Club. Reynaldo felt uncomfortable when they went in and saw so many people in the smoke-filled room. It smelled of tobacco and fried grease. He had promised his client he would be there; otherwise, he would have turned around and left. Reynaldo and Mari Lou walked to the Pérez table and feigned joy. He was exhausted but forced a smile.

In their conversation, Reynaldo spoke about his attachment to the land, knowing how Pérez felt about his two hundred acres. They also discussed each other's family history. In Laredo it was not unusual to be a third, fourth, or even fifth degree relative of Lorenzo Galvan. Good family lines did not guarantee affluence, however. So it was with Reynaldo's parents Adam and Martha García.

Reynaldo's father clerked at the Río Grande Auto Parts, the biggest auto parts store in the city. Martha stayed home and enjoyed sewing for her family but more and more, it seemed, for others as well. They enjoyed their four children, Reynaldo the eldest, followed by Ramon, Reymundo, and Carmen. Supporting the family in post-World War II Texas was not easy, and the children learned early on that they could not get everything they wanted.

Despite their economic problems, Martha had inherited a two-thousand-acre ranch thirty miles east of Laredo. It was a large ranch but not enough to support a family. The family enjoyed weekend outings to the ranch, and the grazing and hunting rent revenue added much-needed income to the family budget. Still, they were "land poor." Keeping the ranch was a constant struggle, but Martha knew the value of having the land and sacrificed to the pay property taxes on it every year.

Her children learned to love the land and appreciated her insistence on keeping it at all cost. This small piece of land helped Reynaldo to understand the feeling the old ranchers had for their particular bit of dirt.

For days after the Pérez trial, Reynaldo caught himself thinking of Mario's threat to appeal the decision. The case did not involve millions of dollars, nor did it affect thousands of people. It was a simple land case, but somehow it went to the very matter of being a Laredoan and a South Texan.

The case made Reynaldo think of his own family. His father did not earn much at the auto parts store, and the extra rent money from the ranch did not help much, which meant his mother had to sew for a little extra money. Martha felt the hardship in raising her children in this situation, but made up her mind they would get the best education possible. This meant the children had to go to the Catholic school in town. The school was not superior to the public school available to the children, but their mother felt more at ease with the religious training the nuns provided.

From the first day Reynaldo loved school, and he made friends quickly. His first-grade buddies included Joe Cavazos and Mario Cantu. Joe's father had a store in downtown Laredo as did Mario's father. They were more affluent than the Garcías or most families in town, but everyone always thought well of the Garcías. After all, they were descendants of Tomas Sanchez; Reynaldo and the other García children were never denied invitations to social events.

During the teenage years Mario, Joe, and Reynaldo became closer and were always together. After school, on weekends, or during social events, the boys almost always could be found at Joe's house.

Joe and Mario's fathers were both college graduates. This was uncommon for Mexican Americans in South Texas, but not unusual for Laredoans. As the boys advanced to junior high school, the talk of college became more and more frequent.

In school, Reynaldo became the principal's messenger boy. Everybody liked the intelligent, quiet, well-mannered young man and he loved the rare opportunity to cut out of class to deliver messages. Being a messenger, he gained access to the students' records. At first, he did not realize what the records meant, but curiosity led him to start opening file drawers and skimming over the information. He learned, to his surprise, that his IQ was higher than Mario's and Joe's despite their better grades. It was not uncommon in South Texas for teachers to favor children from wealthy families or those whose parents were politically well-connected. Reynaldo's family was neither. This newfound information gave Reynaldo the impetus, the desire, the will to go to college and continue his education. If Mario and Joe could do it and if he was smarter, then somehow Reynaldo felt he too would succeed.

By his junior year in high school he was convinced he was going to college, but he never discussed the matter with his parents. He knew resources were tight at home, but he also knew he had to talk about it with his parents sooner or later.

One day when he came home after school his parents were arguing over the extra income the ranch generated, and how it affected their income taxes. They had not set-up a reserve to pay the taxes generated from the ranch income. The house was warm and stuffy, and his father was pacing the living room in deep thought. He was a strong, good looking man with a broad back, powerful shoulders, narrow hips, graying bushy hair, a fair and ruddy complexion. He was above average in height, but not as tall as his son Reynaldo. His father appeared worried as he sat down at the table, scribbling numbers on a piece of paper.

"Martha, I keep telling you, that damn ranch is nothing but problems for us. Every time we have to file our income tax return we are short on money because when you get paid for the grazing and hunting rents you don't set some aside for taxes. I swear, I think we would be better off without the damn ranch, or better yet, selling it," he complained to his wife.

"There is no way we are going to sell it," Martha said with a glare in her eyes. "It came to us free of charge, did not cost a penny, and we are not going to sell it. Only the lazy and greedy people end up selling their inherited land. We are neither. It's true I don't plan for taxes, but somehow we always manage, and we pay them."

"What we really need is for all the boys to go out and start working. It would bring in a lot of extra cash, then we would not have any problems," Adam countered.

"The boys are not going to work full time until they finish their education. And, that is final! Whatever money they make from part-time work is theirs, for fun and clothes, and we can't count on it for our problems, taxes or otherwise," Martha said. For emphasis she repeated, "That is also final! If I have to, I'll go to the bank and mortgage the ranch to pay the lousy taxes, but in the meantime, I am not going to panic. I am going to take in more sewing, and I'll make up the cash, and that will be the end of it."

"I don't know why I try and argue with you. You are so hard-headed," Adam complained, his voice trailing off to a mere whisper.

Reynaldo had walked in quietly and stayed to listen to the entire exchange. He thought there would be no better time than the present to expose his desire to go to college, and get all discussion, pro and con, out in the open once and for all. Then there would not be another horrible argument.

"Mom, Dad, I know you will think this is a bad time for you, but I think we need to talk. I want to go to college," Reynaldo said nervously.

His parents looked at each other in dismay. They were spent from their own arguing but now had to muster up enough energy for another stressful discussion. After a few moments of silence, his father spoke up.

"Look, Reynaldo, I know you want to go to college, but the truth of the matter is, there isn't any money for school. You should stay and find a job and help us with your brothers and sister," his father told him, a voice he intended to sound angry but came across as if he was sorry.

Again, silence overcame the room with only a creak of the floor being heard, as his father paced back and forth in the small kitchen. Reynaldo looked at his mother in despair. Martha, while plump and heavy-set with graying hair pulled back into a bun, was a good-looking woman, with an olive complexion and green eyes. She stared down at the floor as if the used pine boards had a solution. After more silence, she burst out crying, with tears flowing down her cheeks. She sobbed but stopped long enough to speak.

"Reynaldo, I have been taught to hold on to land, especially if it's given to you, or if you inherit it, but I promise you right now if I have to, I will sell it to send you to college. Somehow you will go to college," she said as she continued crying.

Reynaldo knew it was not a good idea to discuss college with his parents, but the matter eventually had to be addressed. Being brought up in Laredo, and in the shadow of Lorenzo Galvan and his forebears, Reynaldo knew the possibility of his mother selling land was remote. She would sooner burn the house down to collect on the insurance. Faced with the dilemma, as he perceived it, Reynaldo had to think of an alternative plan.

* * * *

Every time Joe, Mario, and Reynaldo got together, the talk eventually led to college. They talked about every aspect of it—girls, exams, orientation, dormitories, books, study habits, and sports.

Mario applied to Columbia University in New York. His father encouraged him to get exposure to a different culture, at least for four brief years. The boys didn't know it then, but merely leaving Laredo meant exposure to another world. Mario wanted to be a medical doctor, and the word was, Columbia had an excellent medical school. Joe opted for engineering school and aspired to attend Texas A&M University, the best when it came to engineering, he said. Joe often spoke of joining the military corps of cadets, and how A&M was considered by many the West Point of the South. Reynaldo confessed about how he always wanted to be an attorney, and how he applied to and was accepted at the University of Texas at Austin. He did not discuss the tuition at UT, the lowest in the state, which was a motivating factor in his choice. Of course, the University of Texas had many points in its favor, so it needed no apology.

When high school graduation came, the boys looked forward to one last good summer vacation before going off to college. They promised to see each other during vacations and special holidays like Christmas, Thanksgiving, and Easter.

Reynaldo got a summer job at the Sears and Roebuck to make money for college. Joe, Mario, and Reynaldo saw each other almost nightly, still discussing the new and exciting topic of college. In August, Reynaldo took a bus trip to Austin to visit friends from Laredo who attended the University of Texas.

Reynaldo visited for a week, sleeping at the YMCA. During the week, he walked around the large campus, visited the registrar's office, and walked around the surrounding neighborhood. He asked questions everywhere he went.

On Wednesday he went to the student aid office. The place was small, one desk in close confines of four plastered walls, and a ceiling fan light. One filing cabinet made up the rest of the furnishings. As a matter of fact, the staff consisted of just one employee. Miss Sally Briggs appeared to be about forty-five, was tall, heavy set, with long curly auburn hair, puffy red cheeks, wore pointed horn-rimmed glasses and high heels, and appeared to know it all. Absolutely all. She was eager to help and determined that everyone who sought her help left with at least some assistance. She was the perfect person for the job. The students needed many jobs and positions, but there were not enough to go around.

"You Spanish?" Miss Briggs asked Reynaldo across the desk.

"No ma'am, I'm Mexican," Reynaldo responded. "Oh, except, I almost forgot, uh, er, I am of Spanish descent. My great-great-great-grandfather, was a Spaniard Conquistador, but that doesn't seem to count much anymore nowadays. I'm just Mexican I guess," Reynaldo replied with a confused look.

"Let me tell you honey child, I don't even know what a Mexican is. I know the people down there on East Sixth Street are Spanish, but I never heard this business about being Mescan. Is that really the way it is? You're from Spain, but you came from Mexico, or what? You have got me thoroughly, and I mean thoroughly, confused, child!" Miss Briggs said shaking her head

Reynaldo spent most of the next quarter hour explaining to her the aspects of being Spanish, Mexican, and at the same time being Texan and American. During the conversation, she just looked across the table at the young man, admiring his speech. She took a liking to him.

"Reynalder, let me tell you something, I just love that there little story you told about your great-great-great-grandfather, and your Momma, and yourself. Let me tell you, you're quite a storyteller. And let me tell you somethin else, but just don't tell enny one," Miss Briggs said, as she stooped over the table, her ample bosom covering most of it. "I think you're just cuter than a June bug, and if anybody ever gives you enny kind of trouble you just tell old Miss Sally, and I'll take care of the entire problem."

Reynaldo had found a protector. "Miss Sally" would help him for the rest of his college career.

"When school starts you come see me, and I'll have the best job and deal for you then you can shake a stick at. I promise, I promise, Reynalder. You'll be happy."

Chapter Five

Reynaldo scribbled out his response in the Pérez judgment in his office and gave it to his secretary to type up. He paused, leaned back in the leather chair, and looked up at the diplomas and certificates on the walls. He heard the telephone ringing, and the typewriter going in the background as he started to reminisce about college and law school.

* * * *

The summer job and the nightly rap sessions made the vacation come to a quick end for Joe, Mario and Reynaldo. Before the boys knew it, summer was over, their bags were packed and they were off on a new adventure.

His father had looked at Reynaldo's venture with jaundiced eyes. As far as he was concerned, Reynaldo could do better working and bringing in a little extra cash to help support the family. He realized it was beyond his control though, and yielded to the decision.

"Reynaldo, I know you are determined to go to college, and I don't want to stop you. I wish you the best, my son," his father told Reynaldo as the family sat at the kitchen table having breakfast. He reached for his wallet and pulled out a $100 bill. He handed it to Reynaldo.

"I've been saving this for a rainy day. Today is not rainy, but my eldest son is off on a new adventure. I'd like you to have it," his father's eyes got watery, and he could not talk anymore.

The two of them stood up and the father wrapped his son in a bear-hug, and let out a whimper.

"Dad, dad, you don't have to cry. It's not like I'm leaving forever, or that I've died. I'm just going up the road a couple of hundred miles. I'll be back in about sixty days for Thanksgiving," Reynaldo said, trying to calm his father.

"Uh yes, I guess you're right. It's just that I'm completely new to all of this. I can't remember anyone in my family ever going anywhere for anything," his father replied with a pause, as the two stared into each other's eyes.

His father broke the stare and Reynaldo watched him walk away, and turn for a final comment.

"Reynaldo, I'm not opposed to you going to college, but son, I don't know if I'll ever have any money to send you," he said, biting his lower lip and left the room.

In August 1961, the day finally came. Reynaldo picked up the suitcase his Uncle Henry gave him for graduation, kissed his mother, brothers and sister, and walked out of the house. Joe was outside waiting in his car to drive Reynaldo to the downtown bus station where he took the bus to Austin, arriving at about four o'clock in the afternoon. He thought of going to Miss Sally but remembered she would be gone for the day, so he made it to the YMCA, rented a room and settled in for a restless night thinking about an uncertain future.

The next morning after breakfast Reynaldo walked the unfamiliar streets around the university. There were more trees and grass than he was used to. The weather was cooler. Somehow it seemed as if the cars were newer and different. Students were everywhere. Excitement filled the air. Young people buying books, registering, moving in, renewing friendships. Reynaldo made his way through the campus to the student aid office. He met Miss Sally there, and she burst out with the good news.

"Reynalder, I'm glad to see you again, and let me tell you, I have the best news. There's this little old man, he's an engineer and a self-made engineer at that, and he comes from Italy, and he's been here about five years, and everybody around here is just crazy about him, cause he's some kind of technical genius. Anyway, I'm getting carried away. His name is Mr. J. J. Bonugli and he comes from Sicily in Italy. Yeah, I think I said that already, didn't I? Anyway, you need to go see him at the Physical Plant Building. I'll show you how to git there, 'cause he's got a job for yew. It sounds immaculate to me, I hope you like it. You better go now, and if you have any problems you be sure and give me a holler, ya hear?"

Reynaldo held a map of the campus, and pounded through the asphalt, brick and mortar maze, and made it to the Physical Plant Building about ten minutes later. Mr. Bonugli proved to be the perfect surrogate father, or father figure, any young man away from home for the first time could ever want or need.

"Lemme tell you Reynaldo, I gotta super job for you. You gonna help me keep the English Building clean. All you gotta do is throw out da trash in da afternoons and sweep and mops the classrooms and bathrooms aftah dat. In exchange for dat, you getta sleep in da basement. I make sure you getta paid about twenny five dallah per month. What you think, huh?"

Reynaldo could not believe he found such a sweet deal.

"Mr. Bonugli, that sounds great. I know I can do the job. Thanks, Mr. Bonugli. When can I move in? Yes sir, Mr. Bonugli, I think that's great, I'll do a good job, Mr. Bonugli, you won't have to worry, you'll see, you won't have to worry," Reynaldo said, almost screaming in excitement. He could hardly contain himself.

The pair got into the University pickup truck that the engineer drove and puttered their way through the shaded alleys and lanes. After a dozen turns, and a short drive through traffic, they came to the service entrance of the English Building. They got out of the pickup, and Reynaldo looked up at the top of the four-story building. It was a made of tan brick, accented with orange tile at the top, and had Longhorn and early Texana ornamentation on the stone apron above the last row of windows.

During the rest of the day, the two men worked on cleaning up a large space at the corner of the English Building basement next to the mop closet. Mr. Bonugli directed traffic more than anything, and Reynaldo did the dirty work, sweeping, scrubbing, mopping, scouring, and sweeping and mopping again. He found the mop closet and cleaned it to a shine, and Mr. Bonugli showed up with a small mirror, and a light bulb to replace the one in the closet. With the cleanup, the lamp and the mirror, Reynaldo had a new bathroom, though he would still have to run upstairs to use the john in one of the men's rooms, and he would have to splash bathe out of the mop sink. Luckily, it ran both hot and cold water. If water splashed on the floor, it would flush down the drain in the middle of the closet's orange tile floor.

Later during the day, Mr. Bonugli confiscated a bed, mattress, linens and a pillow from one of the dormitories and topped things off at the end of the day with a massive standing oscillating fan, a desk, a lamp, and a small four tier bookshelf.

Through the years the little corner of the English Building basement was a respectable "apartment" visited by many friends, including boys, girls, teachers, Miss Sally, Mr. Bonugli, and visitors from Laredo. At first, the visitors were apprehensive going to a basement, but after being there five minutes they realized that it was simply Reynaldo's place. Everybody felt at home, and never again thought the room of as the janitor's basement. Through the years, Mr. Bonugli managed to secure a couch, two comfortable chairs, and more bookshelves. Then a small radio, two more lamps, a hot plate, a coffee pot, and other amenities also found a home in Reynaldo's small basement apartment.

Chapter Six

In high school, Reynaldo always got good grades. He realized that in college things were going to be harder. Soon he found out that the hardest was the daily assignments, something he did not always have in high school. Also, the pop quizzes, and there was much more reading in college.

Nevertheless, he adapted and hit his stride quickly. He did his chores at the building as soon as he could in the afternoons and then went down the street to the boarding house where he paid $10 a month for his evening meal. He enjoyed eating with the other unfortunates, mostly young Anglo men from the northern and eastern part of the state. For the other meals, he mostly ate them cold in his "apartment" but occasionally he warmed them up in his hot plate. It was cheaper that way. On occasion, Miss Sally or Mr. Bonugli invited him to eat at their homes. Those invitations did not come too often but were always welcome.

As he progressed in his studies, Reynaldo realized that his courses were not difficult. Early on Reynaldo decided he was going to law school, and he felt it was a waste of time having to take so many courses that he thought unnecessary for a law degree. He was anxious to devote his full energies to learning the law.

By late November, he was ready to go home for the Thanksgiving holidays. He thought of purchasing a ticket on a bus line but decided to hitch a ride instead and save the $14 fare.

On the Wednesday afternoon before Thanksgiving he walked out to the highway, stood by the side of the road, and stuck out his thumb waiting for the first car to stop and pick him up. It was cold and overcast. Though he wore a medium weight jacket, the cold wind blew right through the light weight white wheat jeans he wore. He got so cold his butt started shivering. He laughed, for this was a sensation he had never felt before. He had never been in near freezing weather. Hour after hour he stood listening to the zooming cars and trucks go by. He felt the jolt of the wind blasts the eighteen-wheelers blew by him. He waited. He had thought it would be easy to get a ride, but he was still a brown Mexican boy in Anglo land, and anyone who was Mexican, or looked Mexican, or looked foreign, did not get an easy lift.

After a four-hour wait, a driver in a huge tractor-trailer truck picked him up. By coincidence, the driver was going into Laredo to make a delivery and on his return was stopping in the Winter Garden to pick up winter vegetables going to Chicago. Reynaldo got a direct ride and did not have to hitchhike the rest of the day. That was not always the case. At times he was not picked up and he walked back to campus and tried again the next day.

The trucker dropped Reynaldo off at about midnight and he walked the rest of the way to his house. From a distance he saw his mother through the windows, working in the kitchen. They might have hard times making ends meet, and they might be good solid Mexican-Spaniards, Spaniard-Mexicans, or Mexican Americans, but they were very loyal Americans and always celebrated Thanksgiving. That meant Momma stayed up late Wednesday night preparing the trimmings for a huge turkey dinner the next day.

No one in the neighborhood locked their doors, so Reynaldo walked the three blocks to his home and turned the doorknob slowly and walked in. He was confronted by the smell of sweet spicy odors from the kitchen. He tiptoed to the kitchen and surprised his mother, who turned suddenly and ran to hug him crying all the way. She kept crying as he talked to her and hugged her and lifted her off the floor.

"Stop it, Reynaldo, stop it, you'll drop me, stop it," she shrieked. "Oh, I'm so glad you are home, let me go get your Dad and the kids. They'll be glad to see you. Let me look at you a second," she grabbed his face with her two hands, cried and rushed off to the bedroom.

Reynaldo opened the refrigerator and took out the quart bottle of milk and chug-a-lugged. He looked for more food and pulled out a plate of cold cut sandwiches left over from supper.

His mother came back in a couple of minutes with his father following. His father smiled, and behind him, anxious to get into the kitchen, were Ramon and Reymundo in their pajamas, wiping and rubbing the sleep from their eyes. His father was happy to see his firstborn. He walked up slowly and hugged the big boy, slapping him on the back several times. His father started crying.

"I'm so glad to see you, son, I have missed you so much. How've you been?" his father asked, wiping away his tears.

Reynaldo then hugged his brothers and tussled their hair. His sister Carmen, the youngest of the family, did not wake up for the impromptu celebration.

They all sat down and father and eldest began a long conversation. As Reynaldo gobbled down his mother's cooking, the two younger boys listened wide-eyed and their mother continued fixing the meal for the next day.

The next morning Reynaldo rose early and went out in search of Joe and Mario. They caught up with each other at Joe's house at mid-morning, lazying around the servant's quarters that Joe's parents had converted into an "apartment" for their boys. They all had plenty to talk about. Mario could not talk about anything else except changing his major to political science, and journalism. He did not like, nor want, anything else. Politics was his total life, his total existence and he could not wait to have his law degree and return to Laredo and enter politics.

Joe and Reynaldo were concerned only with what they did on a daily basis, and talked only about the upcoming month's events. They could not see going one year into the future much less a lifetime, like Mario.

After Thanksgiving, the young men met every day, and again Mario dominated the conversation with politics and everything it would take to be a good politician, or work well with politicians. They reminisced about student council politics in high school and how Mario always wanted to be in control. After a while, Joe and Reynaldo began to tease Mario about his preoccupation with politics. Mario understood and backed off and forsook politics for the rest of the holiday which, like most vacations, ended too soon.

On Sunday morning the Garcías rose early and went to Mass at Blessed Sacrament Catholic Church, then returned home for the noon meal. They ate lunch hurriedly, as Reynaldo had already packed and was ready to leave. They all crammed into the family sedan and drove Reynaldo out to I-35 where Reynaldo waited for a ride. They decided to leave Reynaldo alone, as his father had read in a newspaper somewhere, that hitch hiking was almost impossible if there was a car parked next to the hiker, and even harder if there were people around or in the car.

Prior to leaving, his mother walked to Reynaldo through the thick high grass, stopping to remove a grass burr, then hugged and kissed her son.

"Reynaldo I want you to have these $20, for expenses," his mother said while sobbing.

"No Mom, I don't want you to give me your sewing money. I have a job and I'm doing okay. Please keep the money to help the other kids, I insist," Reynaldo pleaded, taking the money and tenderly placing it back in his mother's palm. She took the money and cried openly as the rest of the children and her husband just stared. They said their good byes and drove back to town leaving Reynaldo to hitchhike.

* * * *

The months and the semesters went by fast. Reynaldo kept busy working hard. He could hardly wait to get to law school. He made friends easily, and they often hung out at his small apartment. He had also met a girl from San Diego and they fell in love. Like him, she was descended from the founding families of the small town of San Diego, which was located eighty miles east of Laredo on the road to Corpus Christi. They had a lot in common, including a dislike for politics, so it was not hard for her to say yes to his proposal of marriage. Reynaldo and his Mari Lou had made plans to get married after he graduated from law school and make their home in Laredo.

Reynaldo went home every holiday and summer. He worked at the Sears and Roebuck in Laredo to make money for September tuition and books. He spent every evening either with Joe or Mario, or both of them talking about their girlfriends, business, and careers. As usual, Mario almost always steered the conversation to politics.

Reynaldo enjoyed all of the business courses he took but disliked most of the other required and elective courses. Nevertheless, he realized he must take them, so he studied hard anyway, and usually made good grades. Taking eighteen to twenty hours each semester, time moved on quickly, and it became apparent to everybody that Reynaldo would soon graduate. He applied to the law school, took the entrance exam and waited for the results. He talked with Miss Sally and Mr. Bonugli frequently as graduation approached. With exams over, he had more time to think and he spent that time anticipating the prospect of law school, more than his coming graduation.

Still, he wrote to his mother of the upcoming commencement exercises but told her he understood it would be hard for them to come to Austin for the ceremony. She wrote back telling him she and his father would be there, and for him to please make hotel reservations. "And please don't forget to make it in the fanciest hotel," she wrote teasingly.

A week before commencement, his mother wrote Reynaldo to tell him they would not be able to make it after all. She said she was sorry, but for various reasons, none which she explained, it was impossible for them to be at the graduation of the first in their family to graduate from college. She sent $20 of her hard-earned sewing dollars. Reynaldo cried as he read the letter over and over.

Reynaldo found out from talking to Miss Sally that not all of the students went through commencement, they just went to the registrar's office the next day and picked up their diplomas. Knowing this, Reynaldo decided to cut the ceremony. If his parents weren't going to be there, then he would not be there.

On the night of commencement, Reynaldo went to East Sixth Street in downtown Austin. He took in the *ambiente* devouring Mexican food, guzzling beer, and, indulging in the music. His happiness was sadness. Why did he have to suffer without money, without his parents, when many undeserving did not appreciate either?

Chapter Seven

Reynaldo registered at the law school and found out, to his surprise that he could get a student loan, which would pay for tuition and books and some living expenses. He still had to work some for spending money, but his student loan covered most of his education. He did not have to repay the loan until after he graduated from law school, and the loan carried a low-interest rate.

To his further surprise, while attending orientation for first-year law students, he found assignments posted for each of his courses on the bulletin board. The professors wanted everybody ready to work on the first class meeting. He also learned that the study of law was different from the textbook method used in undergraduate school. In law school, the teaching was done using the case method. Law books did not give a narrative explanation as found in textbooks. The actual case or opinion by an Appellate Court was read and summarized, then discussed in class in the Socratic Method of argument. This meant that at each class one or two students, chosen by turn usually in alphabetical order, were invited to stand, summarize the facts of the case, the legal question tried and appealed, and provide the results or the rule of law. After the presentation, the student was expected to answer questions and argue the case with the professor. Sometimes the discussion lasted thirty minutes.

The case teaching method was strange to all of the incoming Freshmen, but they soon adjusted. Reynaldo quickly took to the law. He loved each of his courses. They were all required, but they all dealt with the law. It was much different from undergraduate school, where one took many unrelated required and elective courses. He acquired a voracious appetite for the law, and read constantly. He typed his notes and his case briefs, something he had never done before. His notes in each course were exemplary.

Reynaldo learned there would only be one exam, that being the final. No quizzes or tests were given in between. He could not believe his willingness to study and his power to read and concentrate. "If I studied like this in undergraduate school I would have been number one in all of my classes," he said to himself.

Reynaldo read that Jews and Greeks made excellent lawyers and were sought out by the large law firms. He secretly made up his mind to change that situation. "Someday Mexicans will be thought of as the best, or amongst the best attorneys in Texas and the U.S.," he said to himself.

His fellow students noticed how hard Reynaldo studied, and this brought some hangers-on who sat or stood near him to ask questions. Most of his fellow students liked him, but others could not stand him but hung around to see what they could learn from him. Reynaldo did not care either way. His efforts were rewarded as he made the dean's list the first semester. He shared the news with his parents and brothers and sister in Laredo and they were elated.

* * * *

Mario and Joe returned to Laredo for summer vacation at the end of every school year. But once in law school, particularly with the aid of the student loan, Reynaldo did not join his friends back home for the summer. He took courses straight through the summer months instead.

He had high aspirations so his studying became more intensive, and it paid off as his grades continued at a high level. His induction into Phi Delta Phi legal fraternity in the fall of his second year in law school came as a surprise. It was an honor given only to students with high averages. At the end of his second year, he also received an engraved invitation to participate in the law journal during his final year in law school. The first semester he mostly helped edit, but the second semester he authored a case note with thorough analysis, retroactive and perspective, of a recent court decision. It was published in the Texas Law Review.

By and large, most of the honors went unnoticed by his family and friends in Laredo. Sometimes he got so busy he did not take the time to explain the honor to his parents, other times he simply did not feel like explaining.

He heard from home, on occasional weekend visits, that Mario was working for the governor of Louisiana. He also heard Mario worked as a law clerk for some of the larger law firms in New Orleans, honing his skills to become a good politician someday. Reynaldo laughed to himself about that. If politicians were supposed to be crooked, and one was a good politician that probably meant one was a good crook.

Reynaldo and Mario missed each other on a couple of the Thanksgiving and Christmas holidays, and only on occasion managed to get together with Joe who had graduated from engineering school and worked for a large real estate developer in San Antonio. Still, the trio got together every chance they could even though it appeared each was going their separate way and that their visits were becoming more and more infrequent.

While in Laredo during Easter of his third and last year in law school Reynaldo arranged for an interview with the largest law firm in Laredo. Of the thirty attorneys in Laredo, only a handful were Mexican Americans. One was an old man who received his degree through correspondence and was on the verge of retirement, another was a partner in the large law firm which Reynaldo looked forward to join, and the others were solo practitioners.

The interview went well. He met the six attorneys, and they all questioned him on his qualifications. His credentials proved impeccable, and the interview ended with an offer of employment. He was given a week to either accept or reject the offer.

The only bad part of the offer was the salary. His pay would only be $500 per month, less money than what he could make at any regular job as a non-lawyer. He mulled the question over and over. The low salary meant he would have to live at home with his parents for a while at least, and it meant that he and Mari Lou would have to postpone their wedding plans indefinitely. He never imagined the salary would be that low. He also learned that he was expected to work hard for every dollar he earned.

He thought about it for three days and discussed it with Mari Lou, but he thought he had a few days to explore any other options he might have. He returned to Austin where he could think without distractions.

Reynaldo was aware of a new social movement that offered a great opportunity for a new Mexican American lawyer like himself. It was called the Mexican American Legal Defense and Education Fund, known by its acronym MALDEF. Reynaldo had met a staff attorney with the group's Austin office and as it turned out he was also from Laredo. His name was Al Martinez. He was six years older than Reynaldo so they really did not know each other, but Reynaldo knew of him. Martinez invited Reynaldo to come by to see him at the MALDEF office on E. Sixth Street so they could get better acquainted over lunch.

Reynaldo looked up MALDEF's phone number and reached out to Martinez. After some small talk, Reynaldo got right to the point of his call.

"I'm graduating from law school next week," Reynaldo said.

"That sounds great, maybe you can come to work for MALDEF when you pass the Bar. Why don't you come and see me? Really," Martinez replied with a sincere voice.

"That sounds great. I don't know if I'm interested in going into a social type law practice, but I was wondering whether you could meet me today. I could really use your advice," Reynaldo said, with a nervous tone.

Martinez said he could not meet until the following day so they made an appointment for eleven in the morning. They could go to lunch after they talked and gave Reynaldo a tour of the office. The next day Reynaldo walked into the nondescript office building and asked for Martinez who rushed out putting on his coat.

"Come on let's go get something to eat, we can talk over lunch, then we'll come back here and keep chatting, let's go," Martinez said as he rushed towards the exit.

Martinez was a large man, but not as tall as Reynaldo. He had light skin, green eyes, and light brown hair. He too was a descendant of Spanish stock. They walked about five blocks to Cisco's Bakery, Martinez's favorite Mexican restaurant.

"Well, tell me about law school Rey, how's it going?" Martinez opened their conversation. While they ate Reynaldo gave him a quick rundown of his law school experience, including all the good highlights.

"Tell me about MALDEF. What exactly is it you do?" Reynaldo asked Martinez.

"Rey, let me tell you. MALDEF is out to right some wrongs. I'm sure you have heard about all the legislation Kennedy and Johnson pushed through on social reforms, and how the government is out to enforce civil rights? That's just scratching the surface. Under the surface, there's a lot of work going on, and it's going to take years, and maybe decades to straighten things out. Ever since the Alamo the Anglos have had their boot on our neck, and it ain't right, things have to change," Martinez said excitedly.

"I'm not sure I understand. Can you tell me more specifics?" Reynaldo responded.

"Sure, Rey. I know what's going through your mind. You think we are just troublemakers and rabble-rousers, and the reason is that you're from Laredo, and you've never been exposed to the injustices that exist in Texas and other parts of the nation. But let me just ask you some questions. How many Mexican lawyers do you have in Laredo? How many of the teachers are Mexican? How many of the telephone company employees are Mexican? How many of the judges are Mexican? Is the county judge Mexican? Is the superintendent of schools Mexican? Are the border patrolmen, and the FBI agents in Laredo Mexican? How many Mexicans vote in elections? Is the funding of the school districts in our state fair, or does it favor the nice and rich neighborhoods? How many Mexicans on state boards and commissions? How many Mexicans sit on the Texas Supreme Court? How many Mexicans sit as district judges? How many Mexicans serve as appellate judges? How many college deans are Mexicans?" Al paused after the litany.

They finished their lunch deep in thought, not speaking.

"I can answer those questions for you if you having trouble coming up with an answer," Martinez finally spoke up.

Reynaldo was dumbfounded, he never stopped to think but the answer to all those questions was either none or very few.

"No, I know the answer," Reynaldo said almost in a whisper. "It's just, wow, I just never even thought about it."

"The big boys aren't going to fold their arms and let us get what we deserve. They are going to fight, and that's where MALDEF comes in. We got a $2 million grant from the Ford Foundation, and we are setting up offices all over the Southwest, and we are going to be available to file lawsuits in whatever court is necessary to correct these injustices. And we are going to need a lot of young, smart Mexican American lawyers like you," Martinez said to Reynaldo, with a wink. "Now let's go on back to the office and we'll keep talking."

They walked through the busy streets talking and laughing.

"Come over down this hall, I want you to meet our director," Martinez told Reynaldo as they walked into the MALDEF office.

"Sit down for just a minute. Let me tell you about Pete Sán-chez," Martinez said, as the two walked into his office first. "Pete is one of the founders of MALDEF. He's been an attorney for twenty-five years. He's done everything there is to do. He's been the only Mexican in many situations, including courts, business fights, school board fights, and elections. He's about fifty years old now, but he hasn't given up his fight. He's smart, and he loves to litigate. I want you to meet him because I have a feeling you'll meet him someday down the road," Martinez told Reynaldo.

"Pete, if I could just have a second, I want you to meet a good friend of mine from Laredo, Reynaldo García. He's graduat-ing from UT law with honors. I just wanted you two to meet," Martinez told Sánchez.

"Yes, hello, Reynaldo, how are you? I know a lot of people from Laredo. Who are your parents?" Sánchez asked.

"My parents are Adam and Martha García, Mr. Sánchez, and it is pleasure to meet you. Al's told me a lot about you, it really is a pleasure," Reynaldo responded.

"Adam García, hmm, doesn't he work at one of the auto parts stores there in downtown Laredo?" Pete asked.

"Why yes, I'm surprised you know my father," Reynaldo said.

"I'm in court a lot and that includes Laredo, and I get to know and meet lots of people. I think I met your dad about fifteen years ago. Well it's been nice meeting you young man, come back and see us, and when you pass the Bar, if you need a job let us hear from you. I have to rush off to the Federal courthouse otherwise I'd stay and chat," Sánchez said, once again extending his hand as he rushed off.

"Reynaldo, come on I want to introduce you to the rest of the staff," Martinez said as they walked from office to office, introduc-ing Reynaldo to the other attorneys, paralegals and secretaries.

Reynaldo thanked Martinez for all his courtesies, and they parted. Reynaldo walked away confused. He had never seen dis-crimination, face to face, and he reluctantly admitted that all the questions Martinez asked showed that Mexican Americans had been systematically kept out of the mainstream. But Reynaldo could not think of fighting the district judge, the administrator of schools in Laredo, or the county judge. That would be his friend Mario's job.

Despite Martinez's offer to help him get a job with MALDEF, Reynaldo was not convinced it was for him. First, it was in Austin and not Laredo, where MALDEF did not have an office. Second, his plans had always been to pursue a business law career. He had a bachelor's degree in business administration, he liked business, and he wanted to put his training to good use.

When all was said and done, Reynaldo realized he did not have a choice. He needed sponsorship in the community or he would never be accepted, and the only way he could get the sponsorship he needed was to go with his first offer.

Chapter Eight

Reynaldo finished the thirty-six-month course at the law school in twenty-four months, but the law required a twenty-seven-month residency, so he stuck around for another semester and took ten extra hours credit he did not need, but that he enjoyed taking nonetheless. He took a familiar route for commencement exercises; he simply did not show up and just went by the administration office to pick up his diploma.

Reynaldo immediately signed up to take one of the bar review courses. Since he no longer attended the University, he could not stay at his apartment. Al Martinez was kind enough to let him stay in a spare bedroom at his house, and even lent him his second car that Martinez seldom used.

When Reynaldo entered the huge ballroom at the University of Texas Student Union to take the bar exam he was extremely nervous. He heard stories of people fainting or barfing throughout the exam, and not being able to finish the test. Some even went to the extent of going to their doctor to get medicine for upset stomachs and tranquilizers for nerves. When Reynaldo heard all this talk he thought it was foolishness, but at the same time, he became concerned. He talked to a pharmacist friend of his and quickly found himself the owner of a huge bottle of pectin for stomach upset and two hundred Valium capsules. Five years later he laughed upon coming across them and discarded both unused bottles.

Reynaldo sat down to write out his exam, gradually realizing that he had over-studied. He was loaded for bear and got a mouse. He felt like he might have wasted time and money in getting prepared, but it felt good leaving the hall, knowing he passed the exam.

Of course, doubt always existed, and it took the examiners two months to grade the exam. He began working at the law firm on the Monday immediately following the bar exam. He got only three days rest before he started. He had moved back home and felt he had outgrown his parents' house, which was only a two-bedroom home. He was uncomfortable living there, but he had no choice; he could not afford anything else.

Reynaldo took to his work with uncommon zeal and surprised the lawyers in the firm. He did not know why they were surprised, as they should have expected a hard worker.

He told his mother to expect the bar exam results and to go ahead and open the envelope, but to call him at the office only if he scored a 75 or higher. If the grade were below 75 she should not call him but should wait, and give him the bad news when he got home. One afternoon, two months after he started at the firm, he got a call from his mother and she informed him that he passed with an 83, and the bar examiners included a note that the highest grade was an 88.

Reynaldo cheered with joy, announced his success to all at the firm. The senior partner at the law firm handed him a check for $100 and told him to take the rest of the day off. He searched Mari Lou out at the school where she had gotten a job teaching English and they planned an early dinner at the Hamilton Hotel's clubroom.

Two years after he started with the law firm, Reynaldo and Mari Lou entered into the Holy Sacrament of Matrimony at San Agustín Catholic Church in the old Plaza of Laredo. They started their life together in a modest two-bedroom, one bath home.

Reynaldo worked hard, and sometimes complained to Mari Lou of nightmares. The dreams dealt with the lawsuits he was working on. At times he jumped out of bed with cramps in his calves.

After the first year, it became apparent that his legal acumen was in property law, oil and gas law, and business litigation. At first, he ended up doing all the small court cases that the more experienced attorneys did not want. That meant that he spent most of his time in court handling divorces and other family law cases as well as fender benders.

The most disappointing thing for Reynaldo was the behavior of judges. The "good ol' boy system" prevailed, and that meant that if you knew the judge on a social or political level, he leaned your way on narrow legal questions, or discretionary matters. Reynaldo quickly came to believe that he had to learn to live with the system. He found himself on the wrong side of discretion most of the time. In law school, students were taught that judges were ethical, impeccable and untouchable, and he never once imagined it would be otherwise. But it was. It was not uncommon to go through a trial, make objections to legal questions and issues, lose the suit, appeal the decision and have the facts over which you objected conspicuously missing.

Early on he decided to appeal several decisions, and obtained reversals. In this way, he believed he would earn the judges' respect, and hopefully discourage favoritism. This meant a lot of extra work, especially when the case dealt with a complex, detailed field of law, but it paid off, as it made Reynaldo a better lawyer, and he proved his point with the judges. They knew that they needed to be straight when dealing with Reynaldo, or he would appeal their decision, and most likely get a reversal.

The months passed, and the firm relied on Reynaldo more and more to handle its cases going to trial. By the fifth year with the firm, he became the principal litigator in the firm. He did not abandon his office practice which now consisted of cases dealing with real estate development, financing, and oil and gas leasing and contracts.

Chapter Nine

During his law school years, Reynaldo saw the stranglehold the Democratic Party had on Texas. He often heard Mario talk about his membership in the Young Democrats but Reynaldo was too preoccupied with school and learning to take an active part in politics. He did consider himself a Democrat; just as everyone else in Laredo.

Discussions at parties and other gatherings found him embracing the liberal feelings of the party's left wing. This was strange because he was attracted to the more conservative aspects of the law, business, real estate, and oil and gas. He reasoned that his family's low-income status, and that of his neighbors in the barrio where he grew up, no doubt pushed him to the practice of law where he felt he could improve his economic situation. But, he could not shake the impoverished images of his childhood in the barrio so by the time he got back to Laredo, he considered himself a dyed-in-the-wool liberal.

After he hired on at the law firm, Reynaldo became an active participant in barrio politics. Most of the law firm partners did not like him getting involved in politics but felt they could not interfere in his private life. The firm was made up of conservative lawyers, but they mostly respected their members' private lives.

Reynaldo got involved in local races, picking candidates on their stands on reform. He felt that long terms in office created rot and inefficiency. He tried to help anyone who wanted to undo the "good ol boy" system practiced in Laredo. He was successful in helping to re-shape commissions, boards, and councils. The older partners took notice, but they rarely said anything to Reynaldo about his politics. One day Reynaldo overheard senior partners Kaspar and Banks talking in the library.

"Shouldn't we talk to him? Hell, he's even stepping on some of our toes, he's moving a little too fast," Kaspar complained.

"Nah, Nah, leave him alone, some of our old buddies need their toes stepped on, and as a matter of fact, they need their butts kicked. They've been in office too long, we need some fresh blood. It's healthy. Don't worry, if he starts causing problems and making waves, I'll sit down and talk to him," Banks replied.

While in law school Reynaldo had met Gov. John Connally at a reception. Connally was then the model of the Democratic Party in Texas, which was to the right of center.

"Hello Governor, I'm very pleased to meet you," Reynaldo had said nervously. "My name is Reynaldo García, and I'm from Laredo."

"Are you one of Tomas Sánchez's kin?" The former Governor asked. He caught Reynaldo entirely off guard. "Who in the hell would know about Tomas Sánchez outside of Laredo?," he thought to himself.

"Why yes sir, I'm a descendant on my mom's side of the family. But how did you know about Tomas Sánchez?" Reynaldo asked curiously.

"Son, when you travel this great state as much as I do, and when you depend on people everywhere in the state to help you, you have to know who is who. If it weren't for Tomas Sánchez, there might not be anyone in Laredo worth knowing," Connally chuckled as he moved on to the next student in line.

"I'll be seeing you around Reynaldo, I promise," Connally winked as he moved along.

Texas had not elected a Republican governor since Reconstruction, and under the conservative leadership of the Democratic Party, it was unlikely any would be forthcoming for many decades. In reality, many Democrats were Republicans in disguise. They knew they could not win elections in the south as Republicans, founded by the Great Emancipator Abraham Lincoln, so they pretended to be Democrats. They could not win office otherwise. When things did not go as conservatives felt they should, they splintered away from the mainstream Democratic Party, such as Texas Governor Alan Shivers did with the Dixiecrats in 1952. Ralph Yarborough dominated the left wing of the party, and almost as a token, it seemed, he was allowed to go unopposed by the conservative side of the party, in hopes it would appease the liberals.

After Reynaldo's return to Laredo and earning economic success as a lawyer, Reynaldo found himself becoming more and more conservative, notwithstanding his ability to mingle and help the local barrio candidates get entrenched in local government.

The day after Easter Sunday in 1978 Reynaldo made a decision to take a turn in political philosophy. It was prompted by a phone call from his accountant.

"Reynaldo," the man on the phone said, "this is Joe Curtin from Smith and Smith. You brought us your financial records for us to do your income tax return. I am sorry to bother you, but I wanted to tell you we are done with your income tax return, and need you to come into the office tomorrow, and bring a check for $2,500. Please bring your wife also so she can sign the return."

"Mari Lou, Mari Lou," Reynaldo called out to his wife. "You remember I told you I hired that big C.P.A. firm to do our taxes, well they must be magicians, they just called and said we only owe another $2,500. I think that's just fantastic."

"Great, honey I think that's great, but frankly I don't know if $2,500 or $25 is good or bad. I just rely on my he-man to take care of us," Mari Lou said laughing.

His brother Reymundo, who was visiting, chimed in, "Hell you lawyers are all like. You make so much money, you don't know what to do except fight to try and keep some of it; $2,500, hell that's what I paid total for all of my taxes, including property taxes, and here you are talking about another $2,500, and happy about it. I just can't understand why that makes you happy."

Later in the day, Mari Lou called to tell him he was wanted on the phone again.

"Hello, this is Reynaldo García, may I help you?"

"Mr. García, this is Curtin at Smith and Smith. We have been going over your return, and we finally finished. I'm sorry to tell you we made a mistake when we reported to you earlier. I'm afraid we will need a check for $25,000, and not $2,500. I'm sorry, and I hope we did not upset your day," the accountant said and hung up.

Reynaldo made a mental note to vote conservatively from then on, even if it meant, God forbid, voting Republican. He was tired of paying for someone else's gravy train.

Chapter Ten

Like most Mexican cities and particularly those in northern Mexico, and in keeping with early European influence, Laredo had a couple of downtown plazas or parks. These consisted of an entire block of land with a bandstand or gazebo in the center. The block was landscaped with huge shade trees and green grass. Sidewalks surrounded the square and crisscrossed from corner to corner and side to side. Before the introduction of television, people swarmed to the plazas after sunset for entertainment and companionship. During the day businessmen congregated in the plazas to discuss business deals, or to get a shoe shine. The plazas were usually dominated by men, and a throng of street urchins insisting on shining shoes for a nickel or a dime, and selling small bags of green Mexican limes. Each small bag held about seven or eight limes and sold for a nickel.

From this milieu emerged a handsome young man named Bernardo Velez whose moxie led him to become the king urchin. Velez became chief of the shiners and green lime salesmen. His distinctive features and similarity to a Greek movie star made the other youngsters call him El Griego.

Velez was a very kind-hearted person, but he learned early on that he should suppress his kindness if he wanted to get ahead on the street, and particularly if he wanted to remain as head of the young pack. It was not just a figurehead position, as he made a penny off of each shine and shared more on each bag of limes that was sold until the lime crate cost was recouped, at which time the commission returned to one cent per bag.

Velez's induction into the U. S. Army during the Korean conflict ended his reign as the Jefe of the downtown plazas. On his return from the Army he began selling used cars and did so well that he soon had a car lot, and then two, then three. His interest did not stop with used cars. His earlier street learning, and his keen nose for the dollar, polished by his Army duty, made him a very aggressive businessman. Velez soon realized that his true interest was in real estate. He purchased lots, held on to them as long as he could, then sold them for a modest profit. On some lots he built homes, small homes usually, and likewise sold them but for considerable profits.

Only one thing occupied Velez's interest more than business and that was politics. Being raised under the shadow of the town's power brokers at the plazas, for years shining their shoes, listening to their talk and strategic planning, made him vow at an early age to someday have strength and power in politics. Of course, his humble beginnings were a perfect entrée with the barrios which were the emerging political centers of Laredo. Just as soon as he could, he dove into barrio politics and got to know all barrio captains intimately. He worked up the ladder also, and knew all the political leaders in the county, and took every opportunity to meet people from the region and state politicians from Austin. Velez was charismatic and people did not easily forget him. Soon, every politician worth his salt was trying to get into the good graces of El Griego from Laredo. His weekly communications included barrio leaders, city councilmen, county commissioners, district judges, and state committeemen. On occasion, he also visited with his Congressman and the Governor. On very rare occasions, but on a first name basis nonetheless, he talked with the President of the United States. The politicians loved him, and he loved them, and he relished being involved in politics.

He liked Reynaldo's style, and by the time Reynaldo had five years of legal experience, Velez was one of his biggest, if not the biggest and most loyal clients. Reynaldo conducted extensive research, examined title records at the courthouse, and determined that there were many fields on the south side of Laredo laying dormant, owned by an absent corporation. The corporation had not farmed the land for twenty years. In fact, they had not done anything with the land for twenty years, except pay taxes.

"Bernie, I just bet if we contact the corporation with a very modest offer, they will jump at it. I feel they've been gone too long and do not fully appreciate the value of the land. They still think of it as farmland, when anyone with a little foresight can see that the future of Laredo lies in those fields," Reynaldo told Velez as he proposed to make a bid on this large tract of undeveloped land. "You can see the homes, the shopping centers right there if you are here, if you are off in Ohio somewhere you can only remember the weeds and ancient furrows untouched by a rusty tractor. Let me see if I can buy it for us."

"Well fine, and then what do we do with the fields? Just sell lots or what?" Velez asked.

"No Bernie, we make a development, a real residential development. I want you to go with me to San Antonio on Saturday and I'll have my good friend Joe Cavazos, who is a big shot architect, show us some first-class real estate developments. Just stick around Bernie, I'm gonna make you a star. Of course, I'll make a small stash of money myself, if you don't mind," Reynaldo said with a smile.

In the following months, the two of them visited San Antonio on many occasions and got some solid ideas. They bought the land as Reynaldo suggested, at a very reasonable price. After clearing the land, and with Joe's help, they hired the best engineers and construction men they could find. They soon laid paved streets, put in a sewer system and street lights, and just like that they owned the first residential development ever in Laredo, Texas. It was three miles away from the Río Grande,

and the river could not be seen, but Velez insisted on calling it "RiverView Hills." Reynaldo only laughed, but the name stuck.

Reynaldo did all the legal work on the project. He determined that the power company would pay for the lights, and even pay to keep the street lights burning, in exchange for a perpetual monopoly in providing power to the development.

Reynaldo masterfully prepared a long-range plan. The catalyst for the development was a little-known law that Reynaldo learned Houston developers were using to good advantage. With their political connections in Austin and Webb County, they convinced politicians to create a Water District. Then they convinced voters to approve its establishment. Subsequently, they convinced the water district board of directors to approve a $5 million dollar bond issue, which Reynaldo and Velez underwrote. As homes were sold, and taxes paid, they were reimbursed, and the district residents themselves paid for their own water and sewer connections and services, and to pave new streets saving them millions of dollars in development costs. Reynaldo planned so carefully that RiverView Hills made them both very wealthy men, and friends forever.

Chapter Eleven

When Reynaldo came back home to Laredo as an attorney, Webb County was served by two District Courts, the 82nd, and the 10th District Courts. As the years passed, it became apparent that another court was needed.

The choice in getting a new court was to add another District Court or following the example of the larger northern cities, to petition the legislature to create a County Court at Law. The County Judge really was not required to have legal training, and the Commissioners Court was not a court of law. The County Judge was the county administrator or its county chief executive, and the Commissioners were its governing board.

The Legislature eventually decided to go the route of a County Court at Law instead of another District Court. The reason for its creation was politics and money. When a new District Court was proposed, it was too hard to get funding, or it was too hot politically to handle. Talk of a new District Court quickly set-off a political fight. State Representative Bob Homan assured the downtown crowd that he would push through whatever legislation they wanted. Instead of creating a battle in Webb County, the powers that be pushed the Legislature to create a County Court at Law.

The problem was not with the downtowners it was with the barrio leaders. Barrio politicians had already begun to exercise their political muscle and voiced objections to the way things were being done and demanded accountability, and representation, a foreboding that went unnoticed until later losses at the polls.

Reynaldo found himself in the position of an arbitrator. Since his return home, he tried to work closely with the barrio politicians. At the same time, Reynaldo had worked in one of the silk stocking law firms. So he was part of both worlds, the perfect arbitrator, the bridge to cover the gap between the classes, between the factions.

The compromise between the parties was a County Court at Law instead of a District Court, and Homan quickly pushed the law into being, and Webb County got its first County Court at Law. The next problem between the downtowners and the barrio political leaders was the judge. Clearly, a downtown Judge would never get the endorsement of the barrios, and vice versa. The County Commissioners were not going to fund the court and court staff, and approve the first appointed judge unless all parties were happy.

Again Reynaldo was called in as a peacemaker, bridge builder, and mediator. He was appointed the head of the Laredo Bar Association screening committee. All attorneys interested in becoming the county's first County Court at Law judge were asked to submit applications and resumes. There were only four applicants. One was an older attorney, who possessed neither the talent nor the energy necessary to launch a new court, find a courtroom site, assemble a staff, set up procedures, and begin trying cases. The other three were younger attorneys, one a woman, also not possessing the moxie to get things done, and the other a barrio rabble-rousing liberal. And then there was modest, make no waves Charlie Zapata.

Zapata was a few years older than Reynaldo and had been three years ahead of him in high school. But Reynaldo knew Zapata well in school, as they played on the football team together. Zapata was tall and broad, light brown skinned, reddish brown hair, a simple face with a hook nose. Despite his formidable stature, he was also never sure of himself, and everyone made fun of him, saying that he was afraid of his own shadow.

After Zapata went off to college, Reynaldo never heard from him again, until he returned to Laredo as an attorney, and found that Zapata was already practicing law there. On occasion, the two talked and reminisced about their football days. Sometimes they faced each other in the courtroom. Zapata still suffered from his high school flaw of not being sure of himself. He walked around chastising himself; "I'm going to get my ass whipped. What am I going to do? Oh, hell what do I do now?"

Still, Zapata managed to get by, and he maintained a relatively comfortable practice. As for being an attorney, he was a lightweight, and everyone at the courthouse knew it.

Although not the smartest and most knowledgeable of the candidates, he was the most moderate, the one that could work with all sides. He embraced no political position or faction. He was honest, above all honest. A knucklehead maybe, but fair, and willing to work hard, and not take sides, and stay clear of controversy.

Reynaldo spent several nights visiting County Commissioners at their homes, or in isolated out-of-the-way cantinas, lobbying for Zapata who he felt was the most convenient choice. Commissioners wanted to meet and interview the candidate. Reynaldo arranged the clandestine meetings with each Commissioner, again in isolated parks and cantinas where the voters could not see them and could not give their two-cents. Several of the meeting places were so dark that it was hard to see each other's faces clearly. After weeks of pushing, the Commissioners Court chose Zapata as the new County Court at Law Judge and provided the funds and staff necessary.

Reynaldo invited Zapata home for supper one night and took great pains to explain to the new judge that he should keep his nose clean.

"Don't take sides. Rule and decide as you see it, even if it means ruling against me. You don't owe me anything. All the people want is a fair and impartial judge," Reynaldo told the new judge. "Don't take too long in making your decisions. Try to be fair and just, and make your ruling, don't sit on it. Above all don't take sides. If the barrios think you are taking sides, they won't vote for you.

"Even if you ruffle feathers and step on toes, that's okay. What people don't like is favoritism. Rule straight, rule right and the rest will take care of itself. Remember that you have to run for election in two years. If the downtowners think you are playing favorites, if you always go against them, if you are not fair, they'll get up the funds to put a candidate up against you. So, don't take political sides. Above all don't let people use you.

"I have gone out on a limb for you, and I have helped you get acquainted, but don't let people use this against you. I don't expect any special treatment, and I don't think you should let anyone else have special treatment."

Zapata said he understood perfectly.

"Oh, I just hope I can do a good job, and don't get my ass whipped." Zapata said, almost as if in desperation.

Zapata performed tolerably well in the County Court at Law and come election time he defeated a barrio rebel attorney. The judge was not a brilliant legal scholar, but he tried hard and worked hard, and the lawyers and the citizens were apparently satisfied.

Not long after the creation of the County Court at Law, it became apparent that the county's growth and the increasing crime and litigation mandated that another District Court be created, notwithstanding that its creation required a hard political struggle.

Representative Homan worked feverishly in Austin to get approval for the necessary legislation to create the court and, as important, to get the State funding for the new court. Calling in markers, and promising future support, Homan got the help he needed, and the 184th District Court became a reality. The only thing remaining now was a judge for the new court.

A downtown splinter group quickly got behind Lorenzo Morales. Offended because there was no discussion, and no attempt even at reaching a consensus, the downtowners met two nights in a row at the Cantina Fenix, a favorite hang-out, and endorsed Zapata to be elevated to the new District Court.

While the local politicos in Laredo were maneuvering to get their man, it was up to the Governor to appoint the first judge, who would then have to run for election at the next general election which was only ten months away.

Reynaldo favored Judge Zapata, although he knew Morales and knew that he was an able attorney. Reynaldo conceded that Morales knew the law better than Zapata, but he was not sure of Morales' ethics, which bothered him considerably.

Unbeknown to Reynaldo, his friend and partner and one-time plaza hustler Bernardo Velez was hard at work in Austin. As usual, Reynaldo focused on the local power players, if he got involved in politics at all. But Velez had his hands all over, from Austin to Washington, and even Mexico City on occasion.

Velez did not waste time. He called Morales in to see him, and the two men and their lieutenants spent several days planning strategy. Morales was very pleasantly surprised to get Velez's support and more importantly, Velez opened his financial chest to him. Velez was one of the county's wealthiest citizens, and everyone knew that money talked.

"Come on in, Lorenzo, come on in," Velez said to Morales as he waved him into his office. "OK, we're all set, sit down. Are you ready to fly to Austin?"

"Of course, I'm ready. Let's go," Morales replied with a wide grin.

"Well, just a minute, I want to make sure that the Governor will see us today as he promised. I've got a call in right now, let's see what he says," Velez said signaling with his hand for Morales to slow down.

The two men chatted about the news and the weather while they waited for the call to Austin to go through. The intercom sounded out, "The Governor on line two."

"Governor, Bernie Velez here, how good to hear from you. I've got you on the speaker, and I'm sitting here with attorney Lorenzo Morales, the one I spoke with you about yesterday," Velez said.

"Oh yes, what can I do for you, Bernie?"

"Well you asked us to fly to Austin today, and I just wanted to make sure that you could see us today. I've got the plane ready, and we can be there in about an hour. What do you think?"

"Well listen, Bernie, I would love to see you guys, but I have some unexpected commitments. Why don't we just talk on the phone. That doesn't bother me if it doesn't bother you. What do you think?" the Governor asked Velez.

"Well OK. We'll do it your way Governor," Velez told the Governor. "Let me lay my cards on the table. I need a favor, and I want you to appoint Lorenzo Morales as the first judge of the 184th District Court, which was just created by the legislature last month. I can't see how it can hurt you politically. For one thing, he'll have to run again in ten months. The only thing is that Bob Homan and his group are favoring another candidate. That's why I'm calling you directly."

"Well Bernie, why don't you and the Homan group try and work things out, that way I don't piss anybody off."

"No, no this is not going to work. Look let me just say this and get this conversation over. I gave you $50,000 for your campaign last time. So now I'm calling a marker. I want Lorenzo Morales appointed, period. Now you do what you think you have to do. I hate to be rude, but we don't have time to bullshit. Help me if you can and if you can't then you won't. OK?" Velez said with evident irritation.

The Governor's voice was shaking.

"Wait a minute Bernie, don't get upset. I understand what you want, I was just trying to be diplomatic. Don't get upset, don't get upset. Look, Bernie, I have my right-hand man looking at this thing closely, and I promise you I'll have something for you by noon tomorrow. What do you think?" the Governor asked.

"Well, all right, but let's get this thing behind us, it's not that big a deal. I'll expect to hear from you tomorrow," and Velez and the Governor exchanged goodbyes.

The evening newspaper the next day confirmed the governor's promise to Velez with a screaming headline reading:

GOV. APPOINTS MORALES TO 184th.

Chapter Twelve

Mario graduated from Loyola University School of Law in New Orleans a year later than Reynaldo. He took time off to work with the Texas Legislature drafting proposed legislation and worked with an Austin law firm that specialized in lobbying.

Two years after Reynaldo began at the law firm, Mario came back to Laredo and started working with a small three-men firm. The two got to see each other more often now in court, but socially they mostly went their separate ways.

"Mario, I hope you don't think you're gonna beat me because I can tell you right now that you aren't," Reynaldo always joked with Mario, trying to psyche him in every lawsuit in which they matched wits.

"I'm not worried Rey, all I have to do is pick up the phone and talk to the judge and get the thing taken care of, and if that doesn't work, then I will pick up the phone and call the appellate judge," Mario replied in kind.

Very unexpectedly Mario began to get a bad reputation within the legal profession. The complaints often heard were, "He does not keep his word. He's always conniving to screw you any way he can. Don't trust him as far as you can throw him." This reputation spread to the business community, the banks, and other institutions. They only dealt with Mario if absolutely necessary.

Reynaldo was disappointed that Mario turned out the way he did, but life went on, and Reynaldo had to think of his own career and family. One day Mario called Reynaldo to invite him for breakfast and said he had something to share with him. They agreed to meet at the Western Motel.

"Reynaldo, I'm going to run for the State Legislature against Bob Homan," Mario told Reynaldo taking him by complete surprise. The two remained silent for a while.

"Can you help me, Reynaldo?" Mario asked.

"Mario, you know I can't. Bob Homan's a big client of my firm, and besides, I think he's my fifth or sixth cousin. I wish I could, but I just can't Mario. Why do you want to run for the legislature anyway? You're practicing law, what do you want to go to Austin for?" Reynaldo asked.

"Rey you know it's in my blood, and I won't be happy unless I'm right in the middle of politics," Mario responded with a twinkle in his eyes.

"Mario you are going to upset a lot of apple carts. Nobody wants you to make waves and upset the status quo in Laredo. Everybody is happy with the way things are right now. You won't be making any friends downtown," Reynaldo warned him.

"I'm not worried about downtown. I have made a thorough and complete study of the district, and I can win whether I can get the downtown backing or not," Mario answered confidently.

"I wish you luck Mario, but I will not be able to help you. I wish I could, but I just can't," Reynaldo told his longtime friend in obvious disappointment.

"But Rey, we've been friends all our lives, how can you turn me down, I'm counting on you to be my campaign manager," Mario said raising his voice slightly.

"You are making me feel horrible, Mario, but there is no way I can do it. Through the years I have formed some solid alliances, and we all have to work together. I can't go back on earlier commitments. You should have tried to work things out first, instead of going for the shock value. I'm sorry," Reynaldo said sitting back on his chair.

"I'm sorry too, Rey, but I'm telling you something, I'm going to win, and you're going to be sorry you didn't back me," Mario responded in anger, as he stood up and stormed out.

Reynaldo sat at the table in the near-empty dining room, drank his coffee, and watched his childhood friend walk away, out of the building. Reynaldo hoped not out of his life.

Reynaldo stared out the diner's window and began to reminisce about the past, the good times, and how times changed. When one is a child or a young man, things take shape and start out on a particular path, and appear as if they will never change. But the opposite is true in life, Reynaldo thought to himself.

Mario wasted no time in kicking off his campaign. He had campaign billboards up all over the neighborhoods before even his formal announcement. Homan was entirely caught by surprise, with no campaign organization, no campaign money, and no campaign platform, no speeches ready, no strategy, nothing.

The senior partners in Reynaldo's law firm brought up the campaign at a law firm meeting and questioned Reynaldo.

"We know you and Mario Cantu are good friends, but surely you must know we are fully committed to Bob Homan and cannot change that commitment," senior partner Paul Banks told Reynaldo.

"Yes I know the firm's business, and I've already spoken to Mario and advised him that I cannot help him. I'll do whatever the firm thinks necessary," Reynaldo replied.

Reynaldo had always been an independent individual and did not like for people telling him what he should or should not do. He had made a private commitment to defend the Bob Homan relationship but did not need to be reminded of it or told that he must back Bob Homan.

The closing comment from Banks, however, made him shudder.

"We don't want you going out and helping Mario Cantu, you understand, boy?" Banks said.

Reynaldo went home in a fury. He discussed the situation with Mari Lou well into the early hours of the morning. He did not like being told what to do, and he definitely did not like condescending references like "boy." They discussed the pros and cons, and they even considered what he should do if he decided to leave the firm. He had never even thought of quitting the firm until that day, but the more he thought of it, the more he considered that possibility. He was convinced that he was out of place in a silver spoon firm.

They talked about Mario and how almost every person downtown, even Reynaldo's friends, disliked him. It came to the point that people commented on how his one special talent seemed to be to get any two people who happened to be together to talk about how they disliked him. He thought privately about how easily Mario seemed to attract dislike, and sometimes even hatred. He seemed to understand that he displeased people, but he seemed to thrive on the conflict. It wasn't just the unpopularity, it was just Mario. Reynaldo and Mari Lou finally concluded they should stick to his initial commitment of backing Bob Homan.

The matter of the denigrating comment by Banks was another matter entirely, and Reynaldo said that he would take care of that at the proper time.

The campaign for state representative got off to a fast and furious start. Mario hit every precinct once per day. Homan was lucky to visit each precinct once per week but he got the downtown money, and billboards went up at last. Mario had his own money and his family's wealth, which was substantial. Mario worked the barrios and the grassroots hard.

The campaign became a portrait of contrasts. The district was composed of thirty counties, and each required much attention and hard work. Homan appointed prominent and middle-class citizens in each town and rancheria to run his campaign. Mario hired only poor barrio leaders. Homan hired a pollster to advise him weekly on the status of the campaign. Mario did not want

to spend money on such lavishness, so he put a new twist on an old trick. In the thirties, forties and fifties, the downtown crowd used political rallies to gather the people, and press the flesh. Beer, soft drinks, and food overflowed. The rallies usually drew hundreds of people and everyone in Laredo was invited. Mario used a similar but different approach called a pachanga. Much smaller than the rally, it involved only one or two neighborhoods at a time which provided Mario the chance to interact with the people on a one on one basis. Mario also insisted that the neighborhood leaders, and not his staff, prepare the food and serve the drinks.

The pachanga was also easier on the budget, as the expense for a pachanga was smaller, and Mario could wait as more money and contributions poured into the campaign coffers to hold the next one. With a rally, the candidate needed a couple of thousand dollars to feed everybody. On the other hand, pachangas spread a candidate thin, but for a young, energetic guy like Mario this did not pose a problem. Mario could cover more people in one hour than the average candidate could shake hands within one night. He moved around with ease from neighborhood to neighborhood, and from pachanga to pachanga.

Reynaldo also had a natural feel for the barrios. Born and raised in the barrio, his perception of the barrio people was something Mario, who was born into money, could not fully appreciate. Mario was just learning barrio politics, Reynaldo had been active in barrio politics for years. For one thing, Reynaldo could talk "barrio" could "street" talk and Mario and Bob Homan could not. Reynaldo could pick up a crowd and in five minutes have them cheering in a fever pitch screaming for action. Mario's technique was to talk one on one with each voter.

Reynaldo was committed to helping Bob Homan, but a busy schedule at the office prevented him from being of much help. During the final weeks of the campaign Homan called a special meeting, aligning all the best campaign workers he knew, and asking for a special last-minute effort to salvage the election. Reynaldo agreed to cover the four northern counties, La Salle, Dimmitt, Maverick, and Zavala.

Reynaldo called in a few markers and arranged for small town pachangas at each of the county seats of the four counties. He coordinated leaders, places, times, speakers, food, and drink. He took extra time at night to arrange all the details.

As the end neared, the activity heightened, and everyone worked a quick pace. Every step was deliberate, and every dollar was well spent. By the week before the election, Reynaldo reported to the campaign manager, in despair, that Homan failed to show at each of the four county pachangas. Other speakers filled in for him. By Election Day it was clear that Homan could not carry the district and that a new Democratic candidate would be on the November ballot for State Representative. Of course, since the Republicans seldom ran opposition, Mario would have clear sailing.

With the civil rights legislation that dominated the early 1960s, including the Voting Rights Act, Mexican Americans worked hard at getting out the vote. Webb County was no exception. In any election, the downtowners controlled and managed to get out 4,000 votes, enough to win an election. This election proved things were now different. Sixteen thousand in the district opted to vote, and Mario soundly trounced Homan 10,100 to 5,800. Reynaldo felt bad about the loss, but he could not candidly admit disappointment.

"I knew he was losing, I just did not know how bad he was losing," Reynaldo told attorneys at the office.

For future reference, Reynaldo was asked to prepare and deliver a report on the election, and the whys, wherefores, and therefores of the outcome. The paper looked like a chapter in a sociology textbook on Mexican Americans in south Texas, and like a page out of Laredo history.

Things were never the same again in Laredo. The "downtown Boys" became a thing of the past, and forever sterile.

Reynaldo could not blame his barrio leaders, they just could not stem the tide of Mario's feverish activity, and Homan's failure to show made delivery impossible. They could not recommend a candidate that did not come around, shake hands nor be seen. It did not matter that Reynaldo himself recommended him. "Where is he? What does he stand for? Why should we go for him? Why isn't he here?" These and other questions could have only been answered by Homan, and he never made an effort.

One thing was clear to Reynaldo, if not to his associates at the law firm where he worked; things had changed and they would never be the same again.

Chapter Thirteen

At the end of World War I, Mexican Americans began to assert themselves in the social and political life of their communities. The founding of LULAC moved the Mexican American community into active participation in seeking redress of economic, educational and political grievances. Returning veterans from World War II sought a more aggressive stand in politics and formed the American G. I. Forum. In the 1960s and 1970s other more politically aggressive groups came into being and Mexican Americans throughout the state began to see progress in their inclusion into the greater society. Faced with many obstacles, these organizations, nonetheless, got the vote out. It did not just occur, it took hard work, and lawsuits and special legislation, but it got done.

One of the unexpected results of the new movements and organizations was the backlash caused by La Raza Unida Party, which was the most radical of the new groups. La Raza Unida preferred the term Chicano instead of Mexican American. Its members were mostly anxious young intellectuals who embraced political confrontation to make their point. The party did not get a stronghold in the border communities.

The border's population was ninety to ninety-five percent Mexican American, and they did not feel discriminated. Through the years, border residents developed a political understanding with their Anglo neighbors. Mexican Americans already held most of the governmental offices in the cities and counties throughout Texas where they were in the majority. The day of

Jim Crow laws, of Mexican and White schools, separate but equal, were over. The days of the Anglo superintendent, the Anglo Sheriff, the Anglo Mayor, or the Anglo County Judge, as shoo-ins was no longer a certainty. Even Reynaldo did not realize this dramatic change, and would not realize it until years later when all offices in South Texas counties were held by Mexican Americans.

In Webb County, the political races were not run on the basis of race or creed, but in the northern counties, political offices were sought strictly on the basis of race. This caused many wounds on both sides, wounds that would take years to heal.

"You know I never thought about discrimination because in Laredo we never experienced it," Reynaldo told Mari Lou one evening while relaxing in the comfort of their living room. "Of course you know about that because it was the same in Duval County. We heard about racism happening upriver, and up north. And, you know the thing is we believed them. In the northern counties, people just like us were treated differently and unjustly. And although we believed the stories, we did not feel their suffering, until recently.

"As much as I dislike taking sides in a racial war, one based solely on hatred, I have to admit, and so does everyone else, that these people, our neighbors, and our blood brothers, had a lot to bitch about. Something I do not understand now is why, now that things are going to be fair and equal, and based on population, and representation, the Anglo populace is not happy. It acts bitter, wounded, and defeated. You know I even heard that up there in Zavala County, the Anglos are selling their land and moving out. I've been up in those areas, and you know it is pretty country. I would not mind living there except for the hatred and racism, and I mean from both sides. It's too bad because it's a really pretty country. I guess someday things will normalize, especially if people learn to leave their kids alone and not teach them hate, bigotry, and prejudice. In the meantime,

I want to stay right here, where there is none. We can all do just fine staying here."

Several months after Mario defeated of Homan, Mario was elected State Representative in the general election, running on the ballot without Republican opposition. Reynaldo and the other lawyers in the office continued to talk about his victory, and the irony of it.

"We all know that the guy is a horse's ass, even if he is your good friend, Reynaldo. He is not a man of his word, and whatever he does, he does for Mario Cantu and no one else. The question is when is the electorate going to find out?" Kaspar said, shaking his head in disbelief.

"Isn't it funny how you think you know a person when you're growing up, then as an adult he's a different person?" Reynaldo said, shaking his head in disbelief.

"He used to be one of my best friends growing up, but I feel the same way about him that you do," Reynaldo replied. "I've had a few run-ins with him, and I can't say I don't wish he were a different man. To answer your question, I think the electorate will figure him out soon. I also think some young buck from San Antonio, which is also in our district, will make a run at him soon. Or Mario will jump at an opportunity for a higher office, and that will be the end of that."

Chapter Fourteen

In the years that had passed since Reynaldo began practicing law, many things changed in Laredo. For one thing Reynaldo was now one of the best and most effective trial attorneys in the county. His clientele list burgeoned. Most of the other attorneys who opposed him knew he was a force to be reckoned with. He did lose some cases, but it was seldom.

For ten years Reynaldo did not take a vacation. Mari Lou became sensitive and upset with this situation, and it became a source of aggravation at home.

"How many other attorneys do you know that do not take a vacation?" Mari Lou asked emphatically, suppressing a scream.

"Mari Lou, you know there are none, and there are also no other attorneys in Laredo that try cases the way I do. None take their job serious, and none work on their cases as hard as I do, and none win as many cases as I do, and that is why we do not take vacations. When I feel we can relax a little, then we will take a vacation, otherwise we do not," Reynaldo replied angrily.

"I don't know what it is you think you need to accomplish, but I do not care if you lose all your lawsuits. What I want is for you to relax with me and the children and take a week or two off. Sometimes I'm sorry I married an attorney," Mari Lou cried and sobbed as she ran out of the room.

Reynaldo stared at the blank wall for about five minutes. He got up and went to the bar and fixed himself another drink. He thought to himself that he had been fixing a lot of drinks after work lately. He felt a slight hunger pang and walked slowly to the dining room, and noticed his place was set. The rest of the family had already eaten supper. Now with Mari Lou gone crying, he would go without supper.

Reynaldo stepped out into the dark backyard. The air was cool. In the dark only the glare from the house lights provided the illumination necessary to at least make out outlines and shapes and direction. He walked to the wooden glider and sat down and began to swing. Reynaldo sat, swung, and thought for a long while, with only the occasional barking of a dog, or chirping of a night hawk interrupting his thought.

He knew the practice of law had gotten out of hand. There were too many clients and too little pay. Many clients felt they could stiff their attorney, and most attorneys were too busy to try and collect. Reynaldo was no exception.

Then, he always worried about the law office management. All of the attorneys at the firm were older than he, and set in their ways. The accounting system was outdated; the equipment obsolete; and the policies, rules and regulations were generations outmoded.

When Reynaldo began his practice with the firm, everything seemed new and exciting. He spent the first few years educating himself on the practice of law and how to apply the law that he worked hard to learn. The experience was new and enjoyable. The next five years, he felt had been an uphill battle, fighting the administration of the law firm. The bookkeeper had been at the firm longer than he had lived. The senior partners refused to even discuss new techniques in bookkeeping, work schedules, library maintenance, salaries and incentives, and docket control filing systems. Things had been the same for thirty years, and the senior partners thought everything worked fine. No doubt nothing would be changed for another thirty years. The new ideas got lip service sometimes, but no changes came about.

"In short," Reynaldo said to himself in the dark of night, "my training from one of the country's leading business schools be damned."

Perhaps he had pursued the wrong career, he thought to himself. The job was good, enjoyable for a while, but now, in what might be called reality, it was not a happy profession. Because of his office's out of date rules, regulations, and procedures it was no longer a happy place to work in. The attorneys were fine people, and he felt indebted to them for having sponsored him in the community. And they treated him well. The cases he handled were the best, the most challenging. He built up a tremendous clientele. For all of this, he could not complain, but he was not happy in the atmosphere, and it did not look like it would change anytime soon. Modern management techniques made it easy and pleasant to run an office, but that was not the case at Banks, Kaspar, and Rodríguez. Everyday was a battle, and everyday brought one or more unnecessary conflicts.

Things would have to get better soon, Reynaldo thought to himself. He walked into the house, and to his bedroom, and noticed Mari Lou asleep under the covers. He got into his pajamas and crept into bed. Someday soon, things would have to get better, he thought as he dozed off.

On Monday morning Reynaldo walked into the law office, requested an impromptu firm meeting, managed to get the partners to join him, and summarily announced his resignation from the firm. He thanked them all for the help and sponsorship, he expressed his good thoughts toward each of them and explained his reasons for wanting to leave. He had stagnated, he needed a new scene, he told his colleagues.

He began cleaning out his desk and thought of all the good times and the bad times he shared at the firm. Johnny Kaspar walked in and closed the door behind him. Kasper walked straight to the window without even looking at Reynaldo.

"You know Ray; I knew this day would come. I don't want you to leave. I tried to tell Paul that things had to change around here. Now that you are leaving I'm sure things will be changed, but it's too late for you. You know the old maxim in business, if you quit, you quit, and there's no taking you back. I wish I could have prevailed upon Paul to change things around here. I'm sorry it came to this, and I hope it won't mean that we can't be friends," Kaspar kept looking out of the window as he talked.

Kaspar caught him by surprise, and Reynaldo felt astonished to hear his thoughts on the matter. He always kept quiet about things, and Reynaldo thought he was the only one espousing new ideas in the firm, but Kaspar agreed with him but chose never to voice his agreement.

"Johnny, you surprise me. I didn't know I had an ally. I'm sorry you didn't speak up earlier, it might have made a difference," Reynaldo said.

"Nah, it would not have made a difference, because Paul would never change his mind. Anyway what's done is done, and I wish you the best. I'm sure I'll see you around the courthouse, right? Be good!" Kasper walked over to Reynaldo smiling and extended his hand. The two men shook hands and patted each other on the back.

"Incidentally, what are you going to do Ray?" Kasper asked.

"You know something Johnny, I don't know, and what's even stranger, I don't give a damn. I think I'm going to take the family on a month's vacation; then I'll come back and put the pieces back together and start doing things. Yeah, I think that's what I'll do. And you know what, I'm not even going to tell the district clerk of my move, which means that you guys will have to try my cases for the next month. How does that sound?" Reynaldo announced smilingly.

"Ray, you can't do that," Kasper replied, also laughing.

Reynaldo arranged for the members of the firm to take his cases for one month until he returned, at which time they would let the clients choose if they would move with him, or stay with the firm.

When Reynaldo got home that afternoon, he was all smiles and bounced into the house, where Mari Lou was preparing supper. When she noticed him, she walked over to him briskly and hugged and kissed him.

"I'm sorry we argued last night Rey, you know that I love you."

"Little Missy Mari Lou, let me tell you the news. I quit my job, and I want to go, and I want you to go, and I want my kids to go with me to a distant place, to a get some air, and think things out. Well, what you think? Please let me know?" He rapped out the message.

"Rey, when you sit down and tell me what you mean, then you can explain this to me, in the meantime just kiss me, and then we'll see" Mari Lou said feigning exasperation.

Chapter Fifteen

After quitting Banks, Kaspar, and Rodríguez, Reynaldo enjoyed his independence. He and Mari Lou bought new furniture, lamps, bookshelves, and office supplies for his new office where he went into private practice on his own. His secretary agreed to come with him, and he hired a younger girl, a recent steno graduate from the Laredo Junior College, to act as receptionist and back-up typist.

The new venture was exciting. He was on his own for the first time ever in his life. He was surprised, when he should not have been, to find that he had a huge following of clients. He always worked long and hard hours, but now it was a pleasure to work late at night, on Saturdays, Sundays and holidays.

Mari Lou was delighted, for the first time in many years. Reynaldo smiled in the evenings instead of wearing a constant frown. He talked with her instead of reading newspapers or staring at the television set. He talked to the children and helped with their homework. Gradually he got so close to his children that he realized he had neglected them in the past years, and he vowed that would never ever happen again. He slowly lessened his grip on the office. He knew that it was more important to be with and enjoy his children than to be a slave to his work.

One evening he sat next to Mari Lou on the sofa, as they watched a news program on the TV he said, "You know Mari Lou, I am such a lucky man. Now I can sit at home with you, and with the children, and enjoy everyone when before all I cared about was sitting at the office and grinding out the work.

It took you to make me realize what I was doing and to stop doing it."

"Well, Rey I always tried to tell you what was going on, but you simply never listened. No matter what I said, I don't think you ever even heard a word, or at least it appeared that you did not hear me," his wife responded.

As the years went by, Reynaldo became a better attorney, acquired more clients, and by budgeting his time better made more money. He was able to spend more time with the family. But before he realized it, he returned to his old habits and was working relentlessly. He became more and more callused and again began to feel unhappy.

Reynaldo usually rose early every morning and read two newspapers by eight in the morning and then worked until noon. Lunch at noon was usually with fellow attorneys, then back at the office for work until six or six thirty. Of course, during a trial or during trial preparation, it meant taking the huge briefcase home or returning to the office, for "fine-tuning," until midnight. Once or twice a week he skipped lunch and played a pickup game of basketball at the Boys Club. When he first started his solo practice he used to play three times a week, and now twice and sometimes only once per week.

One morning, Reynaldo opened the office building, flicked on a few switches, and walked to the rear room, and put on a pot of coffee. He sat at a table to read the newspapers while the coffee brewed. The headline of the San Antonio newspaper spelled it out:

DOWNTOWN DUO ENTERS APPEALS BID.

Pictured in the middle of the upper half of the page was a photograph of his old acquaintance Pete Sánchez with his arm around Roy Pasquel. Reynaldo read the article with interest. Sánchez had resigned as MALDEF counsel about five years earlier, the article said. Since that time he practiced law with his partner and high school buddy Roy Pasquel. Reynaldo could see that Sánchez had not changed much, except for putting on a few more pounds, as the bulge seemed to hang down a little lower. Reynaldo had never met Pasquel, and he could see that he was tall and thin and white-haired. Both smiled brightly.

Among the new wave of Hispanic officeholders, many were friends and acquaintances. The article explained that the law partners were running to demonstrate that since the creation of the Court of Appeals, there had never been a Mexican American appellate justice. They felt this was very wrong. They went on to say that they did not have adequate funding to wage a vigorous campaign but wanted to convey the message nonetheless.

All court decisions, judgments and jury verdicts of the courts of Laredo that were appealed went to the Court of Appeals in San Antonio. Through the following months, Reynaldo kept a close watch on many political races, including Sánchez's. The judicial district covered thirty-two counties, and Reynaldo knew it was very hard for any candidate to cover the district adequately. Reynaldo wondered if the downtown crowd in the large cities of the district were with Sánchez or against him. For his part, Reynaldo had become more and more distant from politics. He knew he was losing power and influence in politics, but he preferred to leave that arena to others, hoping that he would not regret his aloofness later.

As the campaigns came to a close Reynaldo read that Sánchez's opponent died of a heart attack and that his election would now be winnable. The Republican Party had the right to substitute a candidate in place of the deceased, but at this stage of the game, it would be impossible for a substitute to gain any ground, Reynaldo thought. The Republicans decided to let Sánchez go unopposed, and at the general election, he became an associate justice of the Court of Appeals. Pasquel rode his partner's coattails and the two swept into office. Pasquel had been around San Antonio politics for many years and was well known as a rebel spokesman for Hispanic causes, and his aspirations to political office, so it came as no surprise to anyone that he ran for office. What was still surprising, especially to the old timers and the downtown power structure, was the fact that Mexican Americans were well organized and could get the vote out and win some offices. There were many who doubted this in the beginning, but political offices in South Texas were decidedly taking on a shade of brown.

Even though Reynaldo truly enjoyed appellate work he did not have many cases that were appealed. First, it meant an extra and substantial expense, and secondly, the odds against changing the trial court ruling were near impossible. These days he handled about one appeal per year, and had never lost an appeal. It got down to the nitty-gritty of taking the facts of the particular case, and comparing them to existing legal precedent and superimposing each to come up with a comparison. Reynaldo excelled in library research, something that he enjoyed since he took legal research and writing in law school.

On a trip to San Antonio, Reynaldo ran across Judge Sánchez as he walked through the downtown area. Through the years Reynaldo saw Sánchez on occasion and was impressed that the judge had never forgotten their meeting in Austin, when Reynaldo was still in law school, during the formative days of MALDEF.

"Reynaldo, it really is good to see you. How are things back in Laredo? Is everyone doing all right?" Judge Sánchez asked.

"Yes Judge, everyone and everything are just fine. It really is nice seeing you, I haven't seen you since your election, and I congratulate you. I think that is just fine, it must make you feel very proud to be an appellate judge. That's just great," Reynaldo said as he shook the judge's hand effusively.

"Well Reynaldo, thank you for your kind comments. I don't mind telling you that it feels really good. I'm really happy about how things are turning out," the judge said as they walked side by side. "Let me say this, if you have a case in front of me, I'll do everything I can to help you. You understand that."

"Judge, I don't really want you to go out of your way to help me, what I want is for you to be fair. If I have the facts and the law on my side, I don't want to lose, I just want fairness and justice. But I don't want to win just because I know you, or because the color of my skin is brown," Reynaldo said, trying to mask his disappointment.

"Oh, you just haven't been around long enough," Judge Sánchez replied, "You don't think the decks haven't been stacked against the Hispanic all these years? Hell Mexicans didn't stand a chance in an Anglo courtroom. Well now it's our turn, and don't be a simpleton, take advantage of getting even, now that you can."

The judge appeared irritated at Reynaldo's comment. Reynaldo elected not to pursue the matter.

"Well Judge, you do whatever you think. I'm very glad for you and I wish you the best of luck in your new position. I must be off now," Reynaldo shook his hand again and crossed the street in the opposite direction.

He was again experiencing the hatred and bitterness that never fermented in Laredo. He tried to reconcile it in his own mind. He knew, of course, that the stories of discrimination and prejudice were mostly true. He knew about the separate but "equal" schools, particularly in South Texas communities situated away from the border. One school for the Mexicans and one for the Anglos. In reality they were not nearly equal. He knew about restaurants and hotels that refused to serve Mexicans. But none of this occurred in Laredo, so it was hard for him to empathize and become bitter. He thought about the situation for a long while. Finally, he thanked God that he was not born, raised nor lived north of Laredo, or else he might be hate-filled and bitter for the rest of his life. He felt somewhat like a traitor for not feeling the way Sánchez felt, but he just could not muster up the feeling. He knew someday he would be before the Honorable Pete Sánchez and he wondered how the judge would act toward him.

Chapter Sixteen

Embossed invitations were sent out for Bernardo Velez's annual Fourth of July Picnic and they quickly became social currency as a status symbol in Laredo, San Antonio, and Austin. Anyone who was anyone got an invite. Those that did not felt slighted and hated Bernie Velez even more. The River-View staff worked hard on invitation lists and coordinating with caterers and suppliers. Bands were contracted. The champagne and drinks were purchased. Waiters, bartenders, dishwashers, and cleanup crews were hired.

Unfortunately, the day was sweltering. But the heat did not keep the crowds away. The Laredo crowd was going to show up regardless of the weather or other adverse conditions, the question was with the Austin crowd and politicos from Washington, D. C. There was no reason for concern. The out-of-towners came in large numbers. The immediate problem was that not only did they show up, but on the average, each invitee from Austin or Washington, brought three other uninvited guests. The temptation to take a junket to the Mexican border, go across, eat cabrito, get drunk and maybe laid, was too much to resist.

Velez was shocked at the gate crashers. He did not mind the extra number of people, but he did not know if they had enough food and drink for everyone.

"Reynaldo I'm afraid we're going to run out of food and drink. All the out of town people, particularly the ones from Austin, brought extra guests. What do you think we should do?" Velez asked, glad that he was able to find Reynaldo in the large crowd.

"Look, Bernie, we have already spent a ton of money, and I'm not going to spend any more. If they don't like it, they can eat pan dulce. Period. Ni modo," Reynaldo said with a smile. "Seriously, Bernie don't let it upset you. We have done more than we should, we have laid out a good spread, and if we run out, we run out. I guarantee you that everyone will have a good time getting there. Just relax, that's what I'm going to do. See you."

Reynaldo slapped Velez on the back as he walked away. The emerald green grass was soft under his feet as Reynaldo walked around the outside area of the park. People congregated under the shade of the enormous oak, pecan, and ash trees. A southeasterly breeze blew as it always did and, despite the ninety-five-degree heat, provided a cool aura throughout the park. Reynaldo worked the outside area greeting visitors, and Velez worked the area closest to the food. He looked for the Governor, the Lieutenant Governor, and the Senators and Representatives, while Reynaldo true to form was content to visit with his old barrio neighbors from Laredo.

Reynaldo found Mari Lou in the crowd, and took her hand and led her to an oak tree. The two stood up against the trunk and chatted.

"Just look at the size of the crowd, Malu, I bet there are a thousand people here. Boy, those people from Austin sure do know how to have a good time. They are letting their hair down and enjoying the party," Reynaldo said to his wife with a wide grin on his face.

Mari Lou agreed as a young couple from Austin ran by, chasing and throwing watermelon rind at each other.

The pool area had been opened, and most of the young people had congregated there. Reynaldo had warned Velez about the liability question, but Velez had insisted, saying it could not be a July 4th Party without "watermelon and swimming." So Reynaldo had reluctantly agreed, and twenty lifeguards were hired and were directed to strictly enforce the posted rules.

After a couple of hours things calmed down somewhat and the mood, noise, and excitement leveled off to a normal tempo. By this time Velez again sought out Reynaldo and Mari Lou and was escorting them around the entire park area introducing them to all the dignitaries that he could find. One would think it would be the other way around, the lawyer presenting the developer, but Reynaldo had always chosen to remain in the background and let others play major league politics. He liked barrio politics and involved himself in local races, but other than that he rarely got enthused. Velez, of course, was the opposite.

Reynaldo and Mari Lou met the Governor and the Lieutenant Governor. The photographer was at hand to take pictures. Reynaldo and Mari Lou continued to mingle and met up with Pete Sánchez from the Appellate Court in San Antonio, and with him was his running buddy Judge Roy Pasquel of the same court. Judge Sánchez was delighted to see Reynaldo and insisted on introducing him and his wife to the Supreme Court Justices that were in attendance. They walked around until they found five of them.

Reynaldo and Judge Sánchez reminisced about their past history, from the time they had met in Austin at MALDEF headquarters, through the present. Reynaldo asked about Al Martinez whom he had completely lost track of the last few years. Judge Sánchez said that Martinez was still with MALDEF but now resided in Los Angeles, California. They finally parted, and Reynaldo and Mari Lou went on meeting senators, representatives, and other prominent citizens.

The sun finally started to sink in the western horizon, and the park was beautiful. The temperature dropped to about eighty degrees now, which to Laredoans was cool. The dimming fireball turned everything to gold, the shadows grew longer, and the contrast with the green grass and the dark shadows made a perfect portrait. It added to the mood of the party. A perfect finish to a beautiful celebration. Velez and Reynaldo agreed that things had turned out perfect. There were a few things that had run out, but there were still plenty of beans and bread, and beer and whiskey. Enough to keep ninety percent of any crowd happy.

As the sun set Velez's chief gofer walked up to Reynaldo and whispered in his ear, "Don Bernardo would like to see you in his office. And he said to please come alone."

Reynaldo explained to Mari Lou that he had an important conference with Velez and that he would be gone for about half an hour. They found someone for Mari Lou to stay with, and Reynaldo walked the hundred or so yards to the RiverView executive offices. Because of the dignitaries in town, there were official bodyguards everywhere. The Texas Department of Public Safety assigned Troopers and Rangers to care for all of the Texas bigwigs, and some of the national leaders brought their own staff bodyguards. Reynaldo walked through to the back of the building where the executive offices were.

He walked into the room where there was a large, beautiful mahogany bar at the far end of the rectangular room along with six tables between the door and the bar. The walls were lined with mirrors and light pecan paneling. Velez sat at the table nearest the bar with two Anglo men, one which Reynaldo recognized as a supreme court justice. They all stood as Reynaldo approached.

"Reynaldo, thank you for coming my good man," Velez said, patting him on the back. "Let me introduce Judge Troy Turbin of the Texas Supreme Court and his briefing attorney, V. C. Camp. Gentlemen my partner Reynaldo García."

The trio shook hands and exchanged pleasantries. They all sat down, and the bartender came around and took Reynaldo's order.

"Reynaldo I hope I did not startle you. It's nothing earth-shattering, except that the judge here wanted to talk with us. You see gentlemen, I have to pull Reynaldo into most of my conversations because he stays down at that damn law office, and he doesn't come out," Velez said with a laugh.

"You see Reynaldo, Judge Turbin here is running for re-election. He's a Democrat, and he has opposition from another Democrat by the name of John Cardwell from Lockhart. The judge has been on the court for two terms already, and he would like to make it a third, but he has this unexpected opposition, and he wants our help. I told him that we would do what we could. Judge, Reynaldo is a mover and a shaker. He works behind the scenes, quietly, but boy is he effective. Extremely effective."

"Mr. García, I know I have never met you, and there is no reason why you should endorse me, or help me, but I'm here to ask for your help. If you are interested, I could supply a list of the cases on the Supreme Court that I have handled, and I think you will like the legal reasoning and approach that I use and follow. On the other hand, my opponent has been on the Texarkana Appellate bench, and if you review his opinions I think that you will see that he's kind of hard to understand, unstable, not very logical, and not very intelligent," Judge Turbin said, addressing himself to a fellow lawyer. "All I ask is that you look at the decisions and compare them. And I also want to apologize, I did not want to take you away from the party, and I definitely did not want to startle you."

"Oh, no judge please don't worry. I needed to have a break and sit down and rest. I am very pleased to meet you and hear you out. Actually please don't feel bad, I know Bernie here sometimes gets carried away, and blows things out of proportion, but don't worry about that Judge Turbin. I'm very pleased to be here and meet you and Mr. Camp here," Reynaldo said with a smile.

"Well I'm so glad you understand, I was genuinely afraid that you would be disturbed because we took you away from the party," the justice apologized.

The four men talked for about an hour and then decided to exit to the vast park area which was about a soccer field away. They rejoined the hangers-on who insisted on staying until the last drop of liquor was poured. The fireworks display was in full swing and being enjoyed mostly by Laredoans, as most of the Austin and Washington crowd had left for Mexico where they continued partying. The four men enjoyed the cool of the evening and commented on trivial matters.

The relaxed atmosphere soon became the calm before a brewing political storm.

Chapter Seventeen

As usual, Reynaldo arrived at the office early and started a pot of coffee. He opened the windows to take in the cool late October morning. It was quiet outside, activity had not yet picked up, and the street noise was minimal. As was his custom, he sat at the library table and read his newspapers. He started with the Laredo newspaper and then moved to the San Antonio dailies. Halfway through the second San Antonio paper, the phone rang. It was Velez.

"Good morning my good friend Reynaldo. How are you this fine cool morning? I hope you are doing fine," Velez's cheery voice came over the wire.

"Good morning Bernie, we are all doing fine. Thank you. How are you today?"

"I'm doing just fine. Things keep getting better and better here at RiverView Hills just better and better."

"Well that's great, now how can I help you?" Reynaldo asked.

"Rey, do you remember that Texas Supreme Court justice that we met at the bar here during the 4th of July party, Justice Troy Turbin? Well he died yesterday evening, and that leaves a vacancy on the bench, and I have an idea about that, and I want you to come out and let's have a discussion about all possibilities. Can you come out?"

"Yes, I was just reading about that in the San Antonio newspaper. I have to be in court for a pre-trial conference, but I should be done by ten, and then I'll drive on out. How does that sound?" Reynaldo asked.

"Fine, I'll be waiting for you," Bernie said, hanging up. After newspapers and coffee, Reynaldo sauntered over to the 82nd District court and waited his turn for a pretrial conference and by nine forty-five he was driving south to RiverView Hills. He viewed all of the new homes in the development, and he felt a sense of pride. He was a part of it. The growth was beautiful, something to be genuinely proud about.

As he walked up to the building, he wondered what it was that Velez was up to this time. It seemed that Velez had more time on his hands and was always coming up with a new political scheme. Of course, Reynaldo could do the same if he chose not to practice law. He did not have to practice; he did it by choice.

The secretary showed him into Velez's office, and the two men shook hands and chatted for a good while. The secretary brought in coffee. They continued to talk.

"Reynaldo, as I said this morning Judge Troy Turbin of the Supreme Court died. He had already beaten his Democratic opponent John Cardwell from Lockhart, and he had no Republican opposition, so it was to be a shoo-in for him to win another term. He had a heart attack in his sleep yesterday evening, so this sets off a flurry of activity to replace him.

"The rules say that the State Democratic Party Executive Committee, which is made up of about two hundred people from throughout the state, will name Judge Turbin's successor. Incidentally, Mario Cantu is one of the Committeemen, and he is secretary of the committee. I'll come back to him later. Now I have been on the phone for a good part of the morning. I have called everybody, I've even talked to the Governor. I've spoken with Pete Sánchez on the San Antonio appeals court, and I've spoken to lawyers all over the state. I've even talked with several Supreme Court justices," Velez said to Reynaldo and continued his soliloquy.

"My problem is that I'm pissed off. The Alamo happened a long, long, very long, time ago, and we haven't had a Mexican as Supreme Court justice yet, ever. Well, it's time, it's overdue. What the hell, this is the twentieth century. Does the Alamo mean that we are never going to have a Justice on the court? Does the Alamo mean that we will never have a Mexican governor? Just how far is this thing going to be carried? Are we never going to have Mexican officials in statewide offices? This cannot and should not go on, dammit. We're Americans, we were born here, and we have fought and died for this country. Enough is enough. So I have a plan," Velez said, stopping to gain his breath.

"Roy Pasquel, from the San Antonio court, you know, Pete Sánchez's buddy. He says he wants it, and he'll take it. John Cardwell says he should have it because he got the second most votes besides the elected candidate, and the candidate is now dead. He is relying on party effort, party representation, and party 'dues' to get him through.

"Now here is my plan. I have set up a phone bank in the large conference room. We've got ten or twelve phones in there. I want you and me to go in there and call every one of the committee people and lobby for Roy Pasquel. Tell them what we think, and why they should vote to appoint Roy Pasquel. The voting isn't for another three months, and the meeting will be held in Brownsville. So, starting next week I would like for you to come in, say an hour a day, and you and I and the staff will place all the phone calls. What do you say, huh, please?" Velez asked as if it was too late for his friend to say no since he had already set the wheels in motion.

Reynaldo chuckled.

"Damn you, Bernie. You aren't asking, you've already gone and done it. How can I say no? Sure I'll help. Things aren't quite so hectic at the office right now, so an hour or two will be alright. When do you want to start?"

"I knew I could count on you, partner. You sure are one hell of a partner. Thanks. Well, I thought next Monday would not be too soon. At least, let them bury the poor man. Then we'll get busy. I figure we'll call, and have the staff call also, and if there is a hang-up or question that requires us to take over the conversation, we'll be right there. I think that will work," Bernie explained.

"What do you want to do about Mario?" Reynaldo smiled. "You know he says that he's always thinking of his constituents, and is always for the region and that he is always for the minority, and the Mexican American. How do you think Mario will go? You know if we don't pressure him, he won't vote for Pasquel, he'll do whatever is good for Mario. What are we going to do?"

"You are right, if we don't push, then he won't move, he will not go for Pasquel, so I have a special plan for him," Velez said. "We are going to send him a message every day for the next three months, in person, by mail, or by phone call, asking him to get off the damn fence and show his true colors and vote for Judge Pasquel. That will work! If either you or I call him direct, it will not work, but the subtle pressure from outside will work. Of course, before it's finally over, he is going to realize the pressure is coming from RiverView, but by that time who cares? He will have got the message, and I think he will lead the pack if he can."

"Well, we'll have to see. Maybe that will force Mario to do the right thing. We'll have to see," Reynaldo said.

Reynaldo continued working at the office on everything that needed attention, especially the Pérez appeal, as he had come to call the case.

Meanwhile, he and Velez decided that it would be best to make the lobbying calls at about nine-thirty in the morning. This hopefully meant that the committee member had finished his or her early morning meetings, put out any small fires, and was ready to take incoming calls.

Every week Velez and Reynaldo worked the phones and got a mixed reaction. Most were surprised to hear that someone was lobbying for a Mexican-American Supreme Court Justice. Most did not expect it. For most of the committee persons, it caused problems; it was another issue to weigh before reaching a consensus on a replacement. Through the phone calls, Velez and Reynaldo could tell that the Cardwell forces were at work, as most of the committee persons let on that they had already been contacted by the Cardwell people. It was going to be a campaign, and the forces were shaping up.

Reynaldo inquired of Velez every day on the pressure being put on Mario. Velez said the heat was being kept on him all the time. Reynaldo conjectured on the effect the calls and visits would have on his old friend. He knew Mario well, of course, and he knew that he was not dumb.

Reynaldo returned to his office and worked files for the rest of the week. After the first two Mondays, it became apparent that one day per week was not going to be enough, so they agreed to change it to one hour every day. Reynaldo took over the project to put pressure on Mario. He coordinated the effort, talking to people, writing the letters for others to sign, suggesting questions and commentary.

Velez, meanwhile, made it a point to call Pasquel every day and fill him in on the progress of the phone campaign. He never mentioned that Reynaldo was helping. Reynaldo noticed this but did not object, because he did not want Pasquel to feel obligated to him under any circumstances.

The campaign finally came to an end. Reynaldo felt like he had spoken to every Democrat in the state of Texas. He had not, of course, at most he had spoken directly to about sixty committee persons, urging a vote for Pasquel to be the first Mexican American justice of the Texas Supreme Court.

Reynaldo did not even realize that the Committee had met in Brownsville over the weekend, and read in the Laredo newspaper one Monday morning that the State Democratic Executive Committee had met and voted on a Supreme Court Judge to place Justice Turbin. The committee voted 232 to one to appoint Judge Cardwell from Lockhart to replace Turbin. There had been one dissent, and one other nomination, that dissenting vote and rebel nomination was by Committee Member Mario Cantu from Laredo in favor of Judge Roy Pasquel, of the Court of Appeals in San Antonio.

Reynaldo was not surprised. He did not really think they had a chance when they started campaigning for Pasquel, but he did not think they would lose so badly. He thought that the rest of the committee might agree with him and Velez, that it was high time that a Mexican American made it to the court. Apparently, the Anglos were not ready for such a drastic change.

Velez called about mid-morning to discuss the outcome.

"Well, we let 'em know we exist anyway. Apparently, the Anglos did not pay attention to our campaign, but they know who we are and that we are displeased. Whenever those idiots call for a favor, it'll be my turn," Velez said bitterly.

"What I don't understand is the trouncing. Didn't Pasquel do any campaigning of his own? Damn, the only vote he got was Mario's. What about all the people from San Antonio that are on the committee. He could have roped them in. Frankly I feel like a fool. We went out on a limb and exposed our ass and he couldn't mount his own campaign? It's apparent to me that he did not campaign. San Antonio had four votes, and he didn't even garner one of those. Bernie, don't call with any more wild projects, OK?" Reynaldo laughed into the phone.

"All right, I won't bother you with any more of my wild ideas, but let me ask you before we hang up, do you want to go to the swearing-in ceremony?"

"What swearing-in ceremony?" Reynaldo asked.

"Judge Cardwell's of course!" Bernie replied.

"Bernie you are something else. We just got through campaigning against the man, and now you want to go to the swearing-in ceremony? You must be kidding?"

"Hell no I'm not kidding, politics is politics. Just watch me give Cardwell about ten grand for his political kitty, and things will all be OK. Money makes people forget quickly," Bernie chuckled. "After all, they do say that Texas has the finest Supreme Court that money can buy, and I don't think they are wrong. So anyway I am going, and I don't feel bad about it, not one damn bit."

"Well count me out. I don't go for things like that. That's not the way I play the game. I hope you have a good trip, but I will not go," Reynaldo told Velez with obvious disappointment with his game.

"Oh, Reynaldo, you're just too naive. You think you're still in law school, where things are all hunky dory, and on the up and up. That's not the real world Rey, and you should snap out of it and come to reality before you get hurt someday. I worry about you sometimes. Well, I've got to go now, and I really didn't call to lecture to you, so I'll see you. Cheers," Velez said in closing.

"So long, take care," Reynaldo replied.

Chapter Eighteen

Reynaldo was glad to take a breather from state politics, which were too challenging and in the end they mattered little in the grand scheme of Laredo politics and his family's day-to-day needs. It was the local races and politicians that most impacted his life.

No other races had drawn the interest of local actors than the upcoming battle for the judgeship of the 184th District Court. Lorenzo Morales had assumed office immediately after his appointment by the Governor and quickly began hearing cases. The governor would not be involved in his election, that would be up to the voters of Webb County. Morales needed to get as much experience and publicity as possible before he had to run for the 184th judgeship. He desperately needed trial experience to be able to mount a successful campaign.

Morales's patron, Bernie Velez could not help him in gaining court experience but he quickly placed his political resources in motion to help the judge. The campaign kicked off with a big pachanga. The downtowners countered by opening campaign headquarters for their candidate, Judge Charlie Zapata. The bumper stickers, lapel buttons, and straw hats were handed out generously.

The next day, billboards all over Laredo bore a two-dimensional black and white abstract image of Zapata, "El Candidato del Pueblo". Morales and Velez did not take long to play catch up, and by the month's end the entire town's streets, utility poles, and cars were plastered with the District Court battle propaganda.

Everyone got into it with a fervor. The surprising thing was the money that poured into the campaign coffers of both camps. The downtowners did not like Velez, and he did not like them. The residents of the barrios did not like being told what to do by Velez or anyone else for that matter.

"Are you going to get involved either way?" Velez asked Reynaldo, early on in the campaign.

"No Bernie, I'm really too busy. And frankly, I really don't care who wins. Lorenzo or Charlie either one will do fine as far as I'm concerned," Reynaldo answered.

"Don't forget we're partners Rey, after all, we are RiverView Hills, and it would not be wise if you go for Charlie and I go for Lorenzo, now would it?"

"No, it wouldn't. But don't worry, I won't do anything without talking to you first. But you know what, maybe we ought to give both sides a lot of money, that way we will end up supporting the winner, no matter who wins," Reynaldo laughed out loud. He thought it was a preposterous idea, but strangely one that many people followed and might be attractive to Velez, the wheeler dealer.

Velez quickly brought in a public relations specialists and bought media time. Zapata appeared helpless, not knowing what to do. He enlisted the help of his attorney buddies, who turned to the barrio capitanes to get things going. Zapata began meeting after hours with small groups in the barrios. In the meantime, Morales aligned himself with LULAC, whose members were young men, formerly in the grassroots level of Laredo society, but now mostly elevated to white collar and in the middle class.

Zapata had the barrio capitanes running his city campaign, and Morales had the LULACers. Unfortunately for Morales, the LULACers had forgotten their humble beginnings and tried to go for the middle-class vote, a vote that the downtowners had wrapped up for the last ten decades and would dominate for decades to come.

Morales tried to get as many cases filed in his court as possible. The more controversial, the better. He needed publicity. He did land one prominent case, involving the partition of property belonging to a prominent family. He handled it very well, but in the big scheme of the election, it did not amount to very much. It affected only a few families with land. Zapata, on the other hand, had heard and ruled on hundreds of cases in the County Court at Law that impacted the lives of hundreds ordinary citizens. One controversial case affecting a few ricos was not going to help Morales.

The campaign waged on with contributions pouring into both candidates. On a chance visit to Zapata's office to leave some documents, Reynaldo got a first-hand look at the workings of the campaign.

"Reynaldo, I'm happy to see you, please come on in," the judge waved him into his chambers.

"Judge, I'm only here to leave some pleadings, but I'll stay for a moment. How's the campaign going? I don't hear very much in my office you know," Reynaldo demurred.

"Reynaldo, let me tell you, sir, the campaign is going perfectly. I am ahead in the polls run by the newspaper and the radio station and the junior college. I don't see how the guy can whip me. You know something Reynaldo, it's unbelievable, I've collected about $200,000 in contributions! Can you believe that, $200,000! And I understand that Lorenzo is getting just about as much money. Every day it just pours in. Unbelievable!"

"Judge I'm glad things are going so well, as always, I wish you the best of luck. I must go now. I'll see you," Reynaldo stood to leave.

"Oh Reynaldo, don't forget to send in a little contribution, you know every little bit helps," Judge Zapata winked at Reynaldo as he saw him to the door.

Reynaldo put a few feelers out, and even visited a few of his barrio friends during the week, and determined that indeed

Judge Zapata was way ahead of Morales. He really did not care, one way or the other, but he was concerned for Velez and RiverView Hills. Having an enemy on the 184th bench was not good for business.

The following morning he rushed into his office and phoned Velez requesting that they have lunch.

Reynaldo traveled out to Velez's suburban office at River-View but had to wait in the lobby before the receptionist got security clearance to let him into the back of the building and the executive offices. The two men shook hands and hugged briefly in the Mexican fashion. Bernie ordered coffee, and the two sat down to talk. Finally, Reynaldo broached the subject of his visit.

"Bernie, I've got to talk to you about the 184th judge's race. I think Lorenzo Morales is going to lose his britches, and that may mean that RiverView won't have a friend in that court. I've asked around and taken a straw poll, and I just don't think that there's any way that Morales is going to make it," Reynaldo told his friend and partner.

"You know I think that you're right. That man is the laziest man I think I have ever known. I give him the money, I give him the experts, and he still cannot get things to gel. I am afraid that you are right. Well what do you propose?" Velez asked.

"Well early on we joked about contributing to both sides, and I think that the joke is on us. I think that we should give Zapata a substantial contribution to help defray his campaign expenses," Reynaldo suggested.

"You're right as usual. I feel like Judas, but that's politics. Damn that Lorenzo fool! Why couldn't he pan out the way I thought? Before we give a contribution, I want to try something. Do you think you can get Zapata to come out here tonight? I want to try and talk him out of the race. If he resigns and stays in the County Court at Law, then Lorenzo will get the 184th, then we'll be set in both courts, and everyone will save face. Can you get him to come?"

"It's kind of a short notice, and I don't think he will agree, but let me go to work, and I'll call you when I have something to report. Let me get going," Reynaldo hurried out of the office.

He finally got to Judge Zapata at eleven that morning and proposed the late hour rendezvous. Judge Zapata agreed to meet with Velez. They decided to meet at Reynaldo's house and then go from there in Reynaldo's car.

Judge Zapata was very nervous that night. He never was sure of himself anyway, but that night's meeting with the millionaire made him even more nervous. Reynaldo tried to calm him.

"He doesn't bite, just hear him out. See what he has to say and then answer what you feel," Reynaldo tried to calm the judge.

"But what does he want? Do you know?"

"No, I don't know what he wants, but I do know that he won't bite you," Reynaldo laughed.

It was pitch dark when they arrived, and only a few of the offices in the building were lighted. Reynaldo approached the security guard who recognized him. The guard radioed in and was given permission to escort the pair into Velez's office suite.

After everyone exchanged greetings, Velez did not waste time on small talk.

"Judge, I'll get right to the point. You know that I have supported Lorenzo Morales from the very beginning. It has nothing to do with you. That is, I don't have anything against you, and it's only that I don't like those downtowners trying to tell us what to do all the time. That's the only thing. Anyway, I've gone out big for your opponent, and I really would like to see him elected judge of the 184th," Bernie paused, coughed a bit, and lit a large cigar then continued.

"I'll get right to the point. In front of you on the coffee table is a briefcase. Please open it."

Charlie Zapata reached out in front of him, and slid the black alligator case in front of him, and popped the two snaps open.

He opened the top and immediately saw that the lower level of the case was filled with small stacks of $20 bills.

"That's a hunnert grand, and it's for you if you drop out of the race. You don't have to say why you're dropping out, just say you'd rather stay in the County Court at Law. The money's cash, so you don't even have to report it. No one here will ever say nothing. You'll be in the County Court at Law and Morales in the 184th, and nobody loses nuttin. What do you say?" Velez said without a hint of concern.

"Well, hmmph," Zapata cleared his throat. He was never sure of himself and did not know how to respond. Reynaldo scrutinized his expressions. Finally, Zapata responded.

"I don't think so, Mr. Velez. No offense, but I have a lot of people who have put their trust in me, and I'm not going to sell out for any amount of money. I'm afraid not, but again no offense," Zapata apologized nervously.

Reynaldo was surprised to see Zapata handle it so well. Privately he was proud of him. In his own way, the years in the county court at law had helped to mold the man. Apparently, he had picked up some polish. Reynaldo liked what he saw.

The focus was now on Velez, and the old wheeler dealer was not to be embarrassed.

"Well judge I really did not expect you to accept the money, but I had to try. You would have surprised me if you took it. I am pleased that you did not," Velez tried to save face.

"Oh don't worry Mr. Velez, there's no problem. We all have our projects, and some work out, and some don't," Zapata rejoined, feeling more relaxed now.

The meeting ended, and everyone parted.

Reynaldo drove Judge Zapata to his home. The talk was insignificant. The pair talked as if the meeting with Velez had not even occurred. Judge Zapata did not know it, but Reynaldo and Velez planned to give him a $10,000 donation the next day.

Chapter Nineteen

The news reached Reynaldo one week before the election that Judge Lorenzo Morales' campaign had broken apart. Not only had LULAC targeted the wrong voter group, but some of the campaign heads were spendthrifts, who thought nothing of using campaign funds for their personal use. They liberally spread out cash, gasoline, and food amongst their friends and families.

In the meantime, the Zapata operation got sharper as Election Day neared. More and more signs and posters plastered city streets, cars, and lawns. Zapata called Reynaldo and asked if he would be willing to conduct a poll watcher and presiding judge training class for his campaign workers. Reynaldo agreed. He did not want to take sides, but it was apparent now that Zapata was in, and only a double miracle could save Morales.

The poll watchers and presiding judges met at the campaign headquarters in a joyous, exciting and casual atmosphere. Reynaldo showed up in a pair of khaki slacks, a short-sleeved sports shirt, and sneakers. The large group mingled and chatted about nothing in particular.

Judge Zapata appeared and walked through the crowd encouraging his people. Finally, the meeting came to order, kicked off with a short speech by the candidate. Judge Zapata then introduced Reynaldo as their "poll coach."

"I don't think he needs any introduction, as I think most of you know him well, but we are very fortunate tonight to have with us a prominent attorney, who has worked the polls

on many occasions, for many elections, and who always seems to be around when he's most needed. It is with a great deal of pleasure that I introduce my friend and yours, Reynaldo García," the judge roared to the crowd.

The workers responded in kind, with loud cheers. Reynaldo jumped up on the small platform inside the vast warehouse.

"Thank you, thank you. It's good to be here, it's good to be here. Thank you Judge for such a nice introduction," Reynaldo said, pausing for the cheering to subside. When the warehouse became quiet, he started the training.

"I know that some of you have been poll watchers before, and some of you have been presiding judges before. You probably think that you have seen all the tricks and that you're wasting your time at this meeting. Well, let me remind you that there has not been such a heated campaign in Webb County in almost thirty years. As far as knowing or having seen all the tricks—well, you haven't," Reynaldo said with a sly smile.

"I'll start with the old tricks and move up to some of the new ones that I have heard about. Everyone get your copy of the Election Code and let's go over the provisions that allow for your presence in the polling place," Reynaldo told the class.

He then went over the basics, explaining that the presiding judge had all the power necessary to stop any abuse and that the poll watcher had no power, whatsoever. In fact, the poll watcher was just that; he watched. He was only an observer that could record malfeasance or nonfeasance and report the information, which could perhaps be used subsequently in the trial in an election contest. The poll watcher was more of a psychological barrier to misbehavior than anything else, Reynaldo explained.

"Some of you have been poll watchers before, so let me refresh your memory about your role. But those of you that have never served as either poll watchers or presiding judges, pay close attention. Your participation may save the election. Now, most of the fraud deals with people who cannot read or write, and who sell their vote. They walk in and do not know how to vote. To deliver the vote as promised, they must follow instructions as best they can, often with help."

Reynaldo pulled out a shoelace with three knots tied in it.

"This is the shoe-lace trick. Very original name. What the voter does, in this case, is walk into the poll booth to vote. He doesn't know the candidates, and he doesn't care but is there to vote the way someone else wants him to vote. He gets his ballot and stretches the shoestring over the top of the ballot. He knows then to vote for the candidates that are listed by the knots in the shoelace."

The crowd oohed, murmured, and giggled at the simplicity of the fraud.

"Then there is the use of a sample ballot to vote. Just watch for people going to their pockets for a paper or other aid to assist in voting," Reynaldo continued.

"In the meantime, you must be watching the control of the blank ballots. First, most people will not vote against a party in power, because they fear that their vote will be detected and that there will be reprisals against them. So, the first thing you must do is ensure that the ballots are shuffled on the reception table, that the numbers cannot be followed to the list of voters. The next thing you do is keep close tabs of the ballots. If some votes are removed and taken to the back room for someone to write on, they will be stuffed into the ballot box later. Be careful.

"Another trick to watch for is a little known rule in the Election Code. Once the election starts, no one shall leave the poll. I have seen instances where opposing poll watchers ask the presiding judge permission to leave for lunch, and when they return, the presiding judge will not allow them to re-enter. And the judge is following the rules, there is nothing that you can do about it. So be careful. Take your lunch, and stay there, even if you have to pee in your pants," Reynaldo warmed to the crowd, who continued to chuckle at the tricks.

Reynaldo went on for about an hour, explaining the shoe sole trick, the shirt sleeve trick, fake identification, and the rest. He concluded by describing the biggest evil of all.

"All right, now let's pretend that it's Election Day. You have worked hard all day, you have been at the voting booths all day, about thirteen hours. You have been diligent, and your hawk eyes and nose have intimidated everyone into following the law. You are pleased with yourself, you are proud, and you can smell the victory. You have been listening to the counter all day long, and you know that Zapata is way ahead. Now you can relax," Reynaldo spoke slowly and deliberately.

"Now you can relax? Wrong!" Reynaldo yelled out suddenly and loudly. "Think again. You cannot relax, because most elections are lost in the vote counting, than in any voter gimmick that there is. The scenario is this. The presiding judge sits at a large table with all the tally and reporting sheets in front of him. He or she is prepared to start the final count. "For those of you that have been watching the counting during the day, your day of hell might have started early, but for those that participate in the final tally, now is when it all starts. Typically, the assistant presiding judges sit around a table, and together they will fill in the final tally and report sheets," Reynaldo told them.

"The assistant presiding judges start reading off votes, and the judge starts tallying on the sheet. You must be sure that the vote called out is the vote that appears on the ballot. The man can sit there all night and read off votes for his favorite candidate, and not those that appear on the ballots in front of him. So how do you stop it? There is only one way, and that is to get up close to the judge, look over his or her shoulder and make absolutely sure that he reads right. Do not be intimidated by his body odor, nor by his displeasure with yours, get right on up there inches away from him or her, and inches away from the ballots that they are reading," Reynaldo said.

He had charmed the crowd.

"One final thing, if Judge Zapata is ahead, then the opposition will try to pass this information out to the outside workers so they can go find more votes. They'll try to bring them in by the carloads, and try to get things even, so be on the lookout for their workers trying to get information out. Just stare at them when you notice that they are trying to talk to outsiders. Some codes are harder to detect than the spoken word.

"For example, it is common for poll watchers to frequently reach for something high or something low when they see fellow campaign workers come into the poll to vote. If they reach and touch something high, that means that their candidate is doing well if they touch the bottom part of a table or the lower part of a door or window sill or their ankle, that means that their candidate needs more votes. If you see this, it is evident that a coded message is being communicated. Report it.

"That's all I have tonight, if there are any questions, I'll be around for a while. Otherwise, I'll see you here on election night for a victory party. Good night, and good luck!"

The crowd cheered and applauded.

Chapter Twenty

Reynaldo rose early on Saturday and dressed in casual and comfortable clothes. He kissed Mari Lou and the children and was off. It was Election Day, and he wanted to be out on the streets going from poll to poll keeping his finger on the election pulse.

Across the neighborhood, Mario also arose early. He was on the ballot, but had no opposition, and did not need to be out campaigning, but he loved politics and wanted to be out mingling with the candidates and the voters. "Besides," he had told Reynaldo, "you have to keep the machine oiled because you do not know when you are going to draw opposition." So he lent his campaign workers to other candidates.

The polls opened at seven and closed at seven. By six thirty that morning all the poll watchers and presiding judges were at their stations, ready for the opening. Poll watchers registered with the presiding judges, and generally stayed out of the way.

The voting did not pick up until about ten o'clock and continued steadily until noon. In the mid-morning rush, a few irregularities were reported in the south side precincts; Mexican citizens being allowed to vote, and people without voter registration cards also being allowed to vote. The news media picked up on the incidents and blew them out of proportion, and managed to keep people listening and watching for the next few hours. Reynaldo noticed the Zapata workers deliver lunch for the workers at noon, thus eliminating the possibility of forced exclusion by an enemy presiding judge.

He saw the same people providing mid-afternoon snacks. The old Mexican custom of merienda was still alive and well in Laredo.

After noon, Reynaldo drove around with Velez and they heard that Zapata was ahead with a solid two to one lead. Velez cursed his candidate and praised Reynaldo for coming to the political rescue at the end. Morales had the afternoon rush to try to catch up. Several times during the day, Reynaldo and Velez noticed Morales campaign workers hauling voters to and from the polls. Of course, the Zapata people worked just as energetically.

At five o'clock, two hours before the polls closed, the rumor was that Zapata was ahead by a three to one margin. At seven thirty the first count of ballots was released, and a trend was clearly established and did not change for the duration of the tally. The turnout had been massive. Only eight thousand expected to vote, a whopping twenty-two thousand had made their way to the polls. By eight-thirty the radio and television stations had proclaimed Judge Carlos Zapata a winner based on the apparent trend of the counting. The first 184th District Court race was over.

Reynaldo and Velez decided to visit Morales first and express their displeasure at the outcome. An hour later, the pair went to the Zapata campaign headquarters, where the beer, whiskey, and food were plentiful. The warehouse was full of campaign workers, supporters and moochers out for free beer and food. Reynaldo and Velez mixed through the crowd, greeting old friends. Soon they were joined by the winner, who was sipping his whiskey, and reveling in the victory.

"Congratulations Judge," Reynaldo almost shouted above the roar. Velez echoed the sentiment. Judge Zapata motioned to them to follow him to a more quiet area. The trio hurried through the crowd. The judge led them to his offices in the loft of the warehouse.

The offices were not plush but were comfortably furnished, with dark paneling, carpet, and air conditioning. There were three large offices and four television sets. A few of the campaign capitanes were enjoying a late and well-earned supper.

"Come on in here, in here," Judge Zapata motioned for them to follow him into the larger of the offices.

"Sit down, sit down. Boy, what a day. I am dead tired," Zapata said, plopping down on the large leather chair.

"Judge you really showed 'em all right. You blew your opponent out of the saddle," Velez commented.

"Charlie, you did it again. I can't say I'm surprised, because you have always been a very popular candidate. What I am surprised is how little importance was obviously given to the Governor's appointment of Morales to serve as Judge, and I am super surprised at how bad you beat him. I just simply never imagined that you would do so well. What was it about fifteen thousand to seven thousand, roughly?" Reynaldo asked.

"Yeah, that's about it, fifteen to seven, that's close enough. To tell you the truth, I'm very surprised myself," Judge Zapata responded.

"Well Reynaldo, you led me to the county court at law through dimly lit cantinas and back yards, and did a good job for me, what's your advice for me now?" the judge asked.

"Judge I'll give you the same advice that I gave you back during the county court at law days. Just be honest, do not favor anyone politically, and make a quick decision. You cannot please everyone. I told you then, and I tell you now, I don't expect any help in any of my cases in the 184th. All I want you to do is be fair, and don't take sides, no matter who the attorneys are. That has worked for you in the county court at law, and it will work in this court also," Reynaldo preached his now familiar sermon.

"Well, I always tell Reynaldo that he's too naive," Velez chimed in. "In the real world there are many people, and I don't mean those here present, that work by political deals, and that includes courts and judges, and you both know it. Don't get me wrong, I am not advocating dishonesty, I just hope you guys aren't living in a dream world."

Velez stood up and stuck out his hand to bid the judge farewell.

"Judge we better let you celebrate with all your campaign workers and supporters, you have been very kind to let us talk to you privately," Velez said.

Reynaldo joined him, "Yes Judge, you still have a busy night ahead of you, champagne, interviews, and speeches. We better go."

Morales was crushed with the election results. Supposedly, he had many followers, but his showing had been bad. Disappointed and depressed he conceded defeat although it had been apparent since about eight o'clock that he had lost.

In time Judge Zapata took his oath of office and undertook to reorganize the court. He hired his own people and established policies to suit his way of running a court. He had already administered the county court at law, so taking over the new court did not pose administrative challenges. Reynaldo observed the progress of the 184th for any sign of irregularity, and by and large, there was none.

There were a few rumors of minor favoritism, but nothing to cause concern. Reynaldo had learned from experience that too often judges took sides, and "sold out" to friends or political allies. He often wondered if the judges now serving Webb County had the backbone to walk a straight line. He already knew some who did not. One judge, in particular, was doomed to defeat, as it had become common knowledge that he was "for sale" to the highest bidder.

Reynaldo was happy that Charlie Zapata was not a dishonest judge. After creation of the 184th, all cases filed with the District Clerk in Webb County were filed at random. Each court taking its turn on the list. No longer could a plaintiff go "judge shopping."

Chapter Twenty-one

With politics out of the way for a while, Reynaldo returned to his legal routine. The matter of the Juan Pérez case was still awaiting resolution. The Court of Appeals had still not set a hearing date. Reynaldo began to go over the entire case in his mind in preparation for his argument before the Court of Appeals.

* * * *

Pérez's mother had left him a two thousand and two hundred-acre ranch in her will. He was not born on the ranch but from a very early age, when he was able to walk amongst the cows and horses on his own, he grew to love the land. He begged his mother to allow him to withdraw from school when he was fourteen years old. He did not like school and all he wanted was to be on the ranch working cattle, and fixing fences, training horses, and hunting.

After much nagging, his mother agreed to let him drop out, provided he took a one-semester business course. He did take the course, passed with good grades, and began a life-long career of being a Webb County cattle rancher.

Besides the ranch he owned, Pérez also leased land from other landowners that did not care to raise cattle and did not share his affection for working in the dusty low brush. He leased a total of ten thousand acres which, when added to his acreage, represented a substantial operation and provided a very comfortable living.

Pérez was a tall and broad man with a thin almost non-descriptive face. He had tiny slits for eyes and a red almost burnt complexion. His hands were huge and thick, developed from pulling on cattle, ropes, posts, and machines all his life.

He was a conservative businessman who watched his operation closely, worked hard and always managed to turn a profit. He spent long hours in his pastures, sometimes returning home by the moonlight at nine or ten. There were many landowners that did not know the front end of a horse. There were others that knew much about farming and ranching, but delegated all duties. And then there were those like Pérez, who knew all about it, and loved to get their hands dirty in the work the land required.

When his mother died, she left a will that divided her estate equally between her two children. Each of them got two thousand two hundred acres of land from one of Webb County's original Spanish land grants that had been in her family for generations. Her assets were split equally between her two children.

"Look, Minerva here is a map that was prepared in Austin. It shows each of our pastures, and it shows how many acres there are in each of the squares or rectangles or triangles," he had explained to his sister when they met to go over her mother's will. He also showed her the tax statements from the county that showed that the acres corresponded to what was on the map. He told her they could use these documents to divide the four thousand four hundred acres. If they hired a surveyor, it could cost them about $10,000 or $20,000 to get a good survey made.

"I don't know about you, but I would rather not spend that kind of money. What do you think?" Pérez asked his sister.

"No, Juan. I agree with you, let's just use the maps and tax statements. That will do. As it is, my income is not very much, and I don't want to use Mamma's money just to run a survey. You figure it all out and then come to me when you are ready to explain it to me, and then we'll have Reynaldo García draw up a partition deed. That will be fine with me," Minerva had agreed.

And so it happened. Pérez added and subtracted until he came up with an even balance in splitting the large ranch in two. When he finished his calculations, he took the map to Minerva for approval, and then to Reynaldo.

"Rey here it is, we have agreed to do it just like this, just draw up the deed. Give her this part, and give me the other part," he had told Reynaldo, pointing at the map on the desk. They also wanted to leave the minerals alone, without dividing. If minerals were found on Minerva's share, then her brother would get one half, and if there was oil on his half, then Minerva would get one-half.

"We want to share in each other's, just like the old Frenchman did with his ranches when he died," Pérez told Reynaldo, referring to Gilbert Ottani, who was actually an Italian. Ottani established a mineral trust in his will, which came into effect when he died in 1935. The mineral ownership grew into a huge operation. All of his descendants shared in the oil and gas production.

"Well I understand perfectly what you want me to do, and I can do it and I can do it quickly. I just want to advise you and your sister both, that having a survey made is certainly the best and safest way to know how many acres you have and how to divide it," Reynaldo warned his client at the time.

"I understand that perfectly Rey, but we want to save the $10,000 or $20,000 that the survey would inevitably cost. You know that is a lot of money," Pérez had replied.

"I know it's a lot of money, I just want to warn you that you might have problems in the future, that's all. The decision on whether to have the survey made or not, that's your decision not mine," Reynaldo had cautioned his client again and then asked him how much he had in CDs at the Laredo National Bank.

Pérez said he had about $200,000, but that it was his money and that Minerva did not make any money, so that meant she would have to pay from her inheritance. Pérez emphasized to Reynaldo that they didn't want a survey. Reynaldo agreed to proceed in accordance with his client's wishes.

The partition was prepared and Pérez built the few fences required to complete the division. Almost immediately he also made a deal with Minerva to lease her land to provide grazing for his cattle.

Two years into the lease, Minerva asked her brother over to her house and told him that she had some news. He hurried over, expecting some family gossip. He was surprised.

"Juan I know you are going to be very upset with me, but I need the income, and it does not do me any good to own a ranch if my husband and I, and our children cannot live comfortably. So, I have decided to sell my ranch. Because you are my older brother, and because we love you, I am offering you the ranch first. If you don't want it then I'll look for some other buyer," Minerva told him.

Pérez was furious. He liked the rental arrangement because although it did involve substantial cash outlay annually, it did not require a capital-draining mortgage. He should have kept calm, after all Minerva was entitled to her happiness. It was just that he felt she was making waves, and she surprised him with the news.

"No, I don't want to buy your damn ranch, you go ahead and do whatever you want," Juan slammed his fist on the table, stood up and stormed out of the room.

Minerva followed him to the front door.

"Juan please don't get upset, it's not that big a deal and certainly not anything worth getting upset about, Juan please, Juan!!!" Minerva pleaded as Juan slammed the door.

Years later, Pérez called Reynaldo to tell him what was happening with his and Minerva's property.

"Reynaldo I've got to come to see you. This is an emergency. I just lost some of my lands, and I've got to talk to you."

"What do you mean Juan that you just lost some of your land?" Reynaldo asked.

"One of Minerva's fences has been in the wrong place for about ten years, and I just found out, and the guy she sold her ranch to, Larry Flores, is trying to sell my land."

"From what you tell me, I don't see the emergency, whatever happened, it happened ten years ago, or started happening ten years ago," Reynaldo was amused.

"Well to me it's an emergency, please when can I see you?" Pérez asked.

Reynaldo asked Pérez to come to his office the following day to go over this development.

Pérez walked in with long rolls of maps under his arms, and a huge file filled with tax statements and other documentation. Reynaldo was reading his morning papers in the large library, and his secretary showed Juan in. The men exchanged pleasantries, and immediately got down to business.

The table was cleared, the lamp brought down over the huge table, and rolls of maps were unrolled and weighted down, and the other papers spread out on the table. The two hovered over the table like giant buzzards. Pérez began explaining the layout of the land, and the two began measuring acreage. The men worked quietly, only occasionally commenting or asking, or thinking out loud. Reynaldo worked the electronic calculator, ruler, and compass. Pérez used a pencil and paper.

"This map is on one inch to three thousand feet scale," Pérez told Reynaldo. "The metes and bounds on this tract don't close."

Long moments of silence passed.

"Now divide all that by 43,650, and it'll give you the acres," Pérez finally said.

Reynaldo learned his property law from Johnny Kaspar known in the county as one of the foremost property lawyers in the South Texas area. Reynaldo took to property law, and it was one of his strongest subjects. He enjoyed title examination and was very well versed in land measurement. Reynaldo was surprised at how much Pérez knew about land measurement. With Pérez looking over his shoulder, they agreed or questioned the measurements as they went along. Finally, Pérez concluded that a misplaced fence was three hundred feet too far north into his pasture.

"Well, who put the fence there Juan?" Reynaldo asked. "Heck I don't know, I might have even put it there myself, but I don't know. I don't remember."

"How long has the fence been there?"

"I don't know that either."

"When did Minerva sell the ranch to Larry Flores?"

"About ten years ago."

"Maybe now you can see the value of the survey that I recommended when you and Minerva partitioned years ago. At that time you decided that you did not want to spend the money. Do you recall?" Reynaldo asked.

"Of course, I do. I just wanted to save $10,000 or $20,000. Now I know that I should have gotten a survey, and that not having done so might cost me two hundred acres, but there's no use looking back. What can we do about it now?" Pérez asked.

"Let me tell you briefly what the problem is that we are facing. In Texas there are several laws that are called statutes of limitations. There is the three-year statute, the five-year statute, the ten-year statute, and there are two twenty-five year statutes. The way they work is, if someone can squat on your property and prove other elements that are set up by the statute, then that person can acquire title to your property by squatting. This is known as adverse possession. Once the title is perfected by adverse possession, that title is just as good as if the owner had given you a typewritten deed to the property. Do you understand?" Reynaldo asked Pérez.

"Well yeah, I think I do. I've heard of squatter's rights all my life, although I really don't know how it works exactly," Pérez said.

"Let me do this. I'll check some records down at the courthouse, so we can get the dates square, and other information. Then I'll work on these law books here and come up with a report. When I'm finished we'll get together to discuss what I found and the applicable law. Then we can decide what course of action should be taken, if any. You know it might be too late, and there may not be any way to regain that two hundred acres, you understand?"

"Yes, I guess I understand, and that would be awful hard for me to take, losing two hundred acres. That's a lot of land to just lose because of a misplaced fence. Well anyway, get after your work, and call me when you need me," Pérez said, shaking his head.

Chapter Twenty-two

Reynaldo checked the courthouse records and found that Larry Flores had purchased Minerva Pérez's share of the Pérez ranch eleven years earlier. The records showed, however, that Flores had not paid taxes on the extra two hundred acres, nor were the two hundred acres included in the mortgage he took on the ranch. Additionally, he never included the two hundred acres in any of the various hunting leases that he signed on the rest of the ranch.

Reynaldo rented a small plane to fly over the land, and take photographs. The flight revealed that the only improvements that Flores made were possible root plowing and grass seeding, nothing else. Reynaldo called Pérez and asked him to investigate how Flores used the rest of the two hundred acres. The investigation revealed that sometimes he rented it for grazing and other times he grazed his own cattle on it, and on occasion leased it out for hunting.

Reynaldo's research determined that Flores could not claim title under the three-year statute, nor under the five-year statute because they both required a deed or other documentary evidence of the passage of title. In this case, Flores clearly did not receive a deed, nor any other evidence of the passage of title to the two hundred acres. Also, he had not been in possession for twenty-five years, therefore the twenty-five year statutes did not apply. This left only the ten-year statute as a possibility.

Reynaldo read the ten-year statute carefully. It required peaceable and adverse possession, which included cultivating, using or enjoying the land. The peaceable and adverse possession was limited to two hundred acres and they should be enclosed by a good and substantial fence.

Reynaldo continued to read case law and legal precedents under the doctrine of stare decisis, following the common law of England, which Texas adopted in 1845. It was clear that the possession should be open and notorious, and that the two hundred acres should be enclosed, which in this case they were not.

Reynaldo called Pérez into the office and explained his findings.

"So there you have it in a nutshell. In addition, I found this case that seems to help us considerably. *McDonnold v. Weinacht* states that a person who was in possession of a tract of land for twelve years, but only ran cattle on it, and enclosed it with a fence, but did not pay taxes, did not include it in his mortgages, could not 'just hide behind the log' and acquire title by limitation. Occasionally repairing fences and running cattle is apparently not enough," Reynaldo told his client. "In short, I think you have a pretty good case. But I have to warn you, as I do all of my clients, there is no way that I can guarantee the outcome of the trial. We may win and we may lose.

"First, there are many facts that we do not know right now, and we won't know until we take depositions. Second, there is no way I can predict what a jury or a judge is going to think or decide when they have heard all of the evidence in the case. I just want to be absolutely sure that you understand, that it all may be for naught. Also, I don't have to tell you that the litigation will be expensive. It will run several thousand dollars, and it will probably be more than the land is worth. So before you decide, think of all of these factors," Reynaldo cautioned his client.

"What's a deposition?" Pérez asked, catching Reynaldo by surprise.

"A deposition is a proceeding where we sit down in someone's office or library and ask a witness questions under oath. The questions and answers are taken down by a stenographer on one of those little typewriters, and then the reporter puts all the questions and answers in a booklet form. That is a deposition. The deposition can be used at the trial of the case. It serves two purposes. First you discover facts that you did not know, that is, you find out what the witness would say if you were in trial. Secondly, you make the witness tell his story, and then he can't change it anymore. And this brings up another point, depositions and pre-trial matters can get expensive too, it's not just the three or four days that I'll spend in court. There will be many days spent in the library, and in depositions, and digging through records. And I almost forgot something very important, which you are going to hate, but it's a must. You are going to have to survey the ranch so we can prove to the judge or jury how things really are out there."

Pérez grimaced as Reynaldo mentioned the survey. That was an expense he had hoped to avoid for the rest of his life.

"Well, I've already made up my mind," Pérez told Reynaldo. "I know there is no guarantee, but my mother gave me this land, and that Larry Flores took it from me without any right, and I'm not going to lose it without a fight. So get after it. Go!"

"Very well. I'll start working on the petition, and the suit will be filed in about a week. Then a long, slow process begins. It will take about two or three years to conclude the matter. I'll start on it tomorrow."

Over the next couple of weeks, Reynaldo dictated the first draft of the petition and edited it twice before he sent it to the courthouse for filing. He sent copies to the Sheriff's Office so a copy could be served on Larry Flores.

Within a week, Mario called to tell Reynaldo that he was representing Flores and that his client was trying to sell the ranch to a third party, and would Pérez take some money and dismiss the lawsuit. Reynaldo related that the land was something quite special to Pérez and that he did not think that money would satisfy him.

Reynaldo passed on the offer of settlement to his client who flatly turned it down. Land ownership is sacred to most South Texas ranchers, and no amount of money can replace it. Reynaldo heard many ranchers on many occasions express their sentiment toward land. "They ain't making any more of it, and I gotta keep what I got, and get more if'n I can get it."

During the passing weeks, Reynaldo finished his research on the case, focused on its weaknesses and strengths, and prepared a legal brief which he would use as an outline in managing the case. He also prepared other trial documentation, such as the special issues, or questions which would be presented to the jury at the trial of the case. Procedures under Texas law require that the jury may not be allowed to give a general verdict, to determine who should win or who should lose. Instead, the jury is required to return a special verdict, to answer several specific questions which made up the elements of the two sides in the case, the defendant's and plaintiff's. Depending on whose questions they answered favorably, the judge rendered judgment for the prevailing party. In this manner, it was said that the jury was "blindfolded," and it could not be determined which way they ruled.

In the meantime, Pérez hired Alfredo Treviño to conduct a survey of his entire ranch. To begin with, Pérez was required to clear all of his fence lines of brush and cactus, a task that he was not too pleased to perform, because of the expensive labor cost, and because the clearing would certainly reveal that about half of his fences had to be rebuilt. He was a very conservative man, and this meant getting by on a shoestring, not building or undertaking major repair jobs if not absolutely necessary.

It took Treviño a month to complete the survey, and when he finished he concluded that Flores was claiming 201.24 acres that rightfully belonged to Pérez.

Chapter
Twenty-three

Reynaldo filed the lawsuit against Larry Flores and it randomly ended up in the 184th District Court. It did not matter to Reynaldo which court it ended up in, ethically he was not about to ask any judge to favor him or his client. He had let it be known around the courthouse many times that all he wanted was an impartial forum in which to bring his lawsuit and get a fair trial.

As with any lawsuit filed, the attorneys began in earnest to prepare it for trial. This included many pre-trial conferences with the judge who monitored the progress of the preparation. Preparing also meant taking every witnesses' deposition. Under modern trial practice rules, the parties were entitled to find out what the other's case was all about, and it was rare that an attorney was surprised by anything at the trial. Reynaldo took depositions from Larry Flores, Juan Pérez, Alfredo Treviño, several landowners with property adjacent to the Flores ranch, Minerva Pérez García, and former Flores ranch hand and current tenant Pepe Reyna. The depositions took months to complete, and at each juncture, the attorneys researched the law some more, and when necessary filed additional pleadings in the lawsuit.

Pérez and Reynaldo had continued to investigate the facts surrounding the possession by Flores. After dozens of phone calls, they found Reyna, Flores' old ranch hand who had worked for Flores for eight years, and now worked at a car repair shop in Laredo.

Reyna invited Reynaldo to come to his home after work and they could talk in private.

"Only because I have known Juan Pérez all my life and because I consider him to be a very good friend, but if it weren't for that I would not talk to you," Reyna told Reynaldo. "You see I am leasing that land right now, and if I say something that doesn't help Mr. Larry, or that doesn't help the new buyer, then I lose the land and have to sell my cows, you see, because I have no big ranch like Juan Pérez, you see. But it is OK, I talk to you. You just come on over anytime, and we talk."

Reynaldo drove through the dark barrio streets until he found the small house. The two men spoke for about an hour.

Reyna told Reynaldo that Flores always spoke of owning only two thousand two hundred acres, never claiming more land than what he bought from Doña Minerva. Reyna added that the only use Flores ever put the property to was cattle ranching, and occasionally leasing the ranch out for hunting. He explained that the two hundred acres in contention were not enclosed by a separate fence.

The interview with Reyna revealed a slightly different angle to Flores' story. Reyna alleged that Flores had told him that the ranch was two thousand two hundred acres, but that the payment would be a gross figure of $4,800 per year, which calculated at the usual rate of $2 per acre rate for two thousand four hundred acres.

"He told me 'take it or leave it,'" Reyna said. So Flores was charging for the two thousand four hundred acres, two hundred acres more than what he said he owned.

Reynaldo next took his investigation to the local United States Soil Conservation Service and found out that Flores never claimed more than two thousand two hundred acres, and never applied for their assistance in improving the two hundred acres that were in dispute.

Reynaldo tried several times to take Flores' deposition, but Mario always called to make excuses and postponed the session. Reynaldo knew that he could take the testimony at any time if he forced the issue, but he waited for the right time.

The day finally came to take Flores' deposition. Flores sat in Reynaldo's law library, in front of a stenographer, with Mario at his side, and Reynaldo and Pérez across the table. Flores was an obese man of medium height. He barely fit in the wooden captain's chair, and rolls of blubber formed around his waist. His small pinhead looked funny on such a large body. His hair was black, straight, and unmanageable. He wore glasses as he sat nervously wringing his hands with sweat beads forming on his forehead and around his lips.

"Do you swear to tell the truth, the whole truth, and nothing but the truth, so help you God?" the stenographer formally asked Flores.

"I do," Flores said, almost choking.

The small group sat at the large table, surrounded by law books. It was quiet. The room was frigid. Flores, nevertheless, perspired heavily. Reynaldo asked preliminary questions, name, address, marital status, and then explained the deposition.

"It is exactly as if we were in court right now, and the judge and jury are watching you testify. At the time of the trial I can and probably will use this deposition. Do you understand that?"

"I do understand that," Flores answered.

Reynaldo then moved into the specific questions.

"Have you ever paid taxes on this particular two hundred acre tract of land?"

"No, I have not," Flores replied.

After an awkward pause, the interview continued.

"I'll show you what has been marked as exhibits two and three, and advise you that these are mortgages that you entered into with the State Bank and Trust here in Laredo. I ask you now if you ever mortgaged the subject two hundred acres?"

"No, I never did."

"Did you ever tell anyone that you were claiming those two hundred acres?"

"No, I never did."

"Did you ever do anything on the two hundred acres other than run cattle on them?"

"No, I did not except fixing the fences occasionally."

"Did you ever tell Pepe Reyna that you were leasing him two thousand and four hundred acres?"

"No, I did not."

"When did you find out that you had an extra two hundred acres that you did not buy from Minerva Pérez García?"

"Oh, I found out almost immediately. I had a survey made one month after I bought the ranch, and it showed very clearly that I got an extra two hundred acres," Flores tentatively answered.

Reynaldo was not prepared for the answer, in fact, he was shocked by it.

"How much did the survey cost you?"

"It cost $20,000."

"And you knew right away that you got another two hundred acres that you did not bargain for, and that you did not pay for?" Reynaldo asked loudly and emphatically.

"Well my attorney says I bought her ranch, and that includes everything that comes with it."

"But you knew you did not bargain for the extra two hundred acres, didn't you?"

"Yes, I knew."

"Didn't you feel like you were stealing two hundred acres? Getting something that you didn't buy and pay for?"

"No. My attorney told me I bought the whole ranch."

"Did you do anything to tell the world that you were claiming the extra two hundred acres?"

"I just did what my attorney told me to do, which was just to fix the fences."

"And who was the attorney that gave you this advice?"

"It was Mario Cantu."

"And did your attorney tell you to pay taxes on the property?"

"Yes, he did."

"And did your attorney tell you to claim the property against everyone, and to tell everyone that you owned it?"

"Yes, he did."

"But you did not, did you?"

"No, I did not."

"And why not?"

"Because I knew that Juan Pérez would bring a lawsuit, and maybe I would lose it."

Reynaldo fumed.

"I don't have any other questions, I'll reserve other questions to the time of trial. We're off the record now. Please leave my office now, I don't enjoy having people like you here," Reynaldo told Flores.

Mario and Flores picked up and began to leave.

"Reynaldo doesn't take these things personally, it's only a job," Mario said to his client, as they left, trying to pacify the matter.

"Aw hell, man. You're just as bad as he is. Now, both of you get the hell outta my office, I'll take care of you in court," Reynaldo told them.

The two men left, and Pérez sat nervously looking at his attorney, not knowing what to expect.

"What a son of a bitch!" Reynaldo screamed. "He knew immediately he got the two hundred acres, and tried to go into adverse possession to screw you out of your land. Sometimes I wonder if it wasn't easier a hundred years ago. If we lived then, I would have shot Larry Flores myself. What a slimy, repulsive bastard," Reynaldo continued, finally stopping, removing his glasses, and massaging his face with his open hands.

"Now we need to get ready for trial. We try the case in sixty days. Are you ready?"

"Yeah, hell yeah, I'm ready," his client answered.

"Well fine, just don't forget there are no guarantees. I can't forecast where we're going in this case. I think we have one hell of a chance at winning but nothing's for sure anymore. You understand that, don't you?"

"Yeah I understand, but let's get after 'em."

****

Judge Zapata, set aside the first two weeks of each month for jury trials. Only the cases ready with depositions, trial briefs, jury questions, and other pleadings were entitled to go to trial. Following this guideline, the court clerk gave each case a number or priority, and it was not uncommon for ten cases to be set for jury selection on a Monday. The practical effect of this was that only one or two cases could be tried, and the balance were passed to the following months, or subsequent term.

All of this spelled delay, and additional time spent on the case following the procedure through the court system. Pérez was not pleased with either the delay or the additional time spent on the case, which meant additional attorney's fees. He visited Reynaldo at his office early one morning. The two men sat in the library sipping coffee.

"Reynaldo, I wish this thing was over. Sometimes I wake up at night, and I've just had a nightmare where I was choking Larry Flores to death. Or at other times, I just walk up to him and shoot him. Some nights I just dream, it seems, about the depositions I have attended, and I imagine myself in court. The truth of the matter is that I am sick all the time. It feels as if adrenalin is in my body, in my neck, in my face, in my chest, at all times. You know, when I was a kid I felt that way whenever I got into a fight, but then after the fight it would go away. Well now, it won't go away. I just don't know how you do it with all these lawsuits you lawyers handle."

Pérez took a deep breath and exhaled loudly.

"I wonder if there is any way you can learn to relax if you are in a lawsuit. I mean how can you learn to fight constantly? Maybe if I teach my kids to fight once a week for the rest of their lives, they'll build up a shell and then when they grow up they won't feel any anxiety when they have to fight in court or in other areas. Anyway, I don't know what the answer is, but I just wish that this suit was over and done with," Pérez told his attorney.

Reynaldo explained to Pérez that his feelings were shared. He had spoken on the same topic with many of his clients, and those that were not used to litigating and that did not participate in aggressive negotiating or behavior frequently, often felt at a disadvantage in litigation. The only comfort Reynaldo offered his client was that Flores probably felt doubly anxious, being as he had indeed stolen the property, knowing he did not buy it, and still claiming it now under a special law. The two men had already seen how he behaved at his deposition. It looked as if Flores were going to have a heart attack.

The anxiety was not the only thing that bothered Pérez.

"Also, I've been looking at your bills. You know I think your fees are more than the land is worth. I should have let him have it without a fight."

"Hey wait a minute," Reynaldo demanded as he grinned. "I told you from the very beginning that it was going to be a costly proposition, and I believe you responded that it was a matter of principle and that you had the money anyway, and you couldn't take the money with you. As a matter of fact, my friend, right after we talked I dictated a letter repeating what I had expressed to you orally, and here is a copy of the letter."

Reynaldo reached into the file, withdrew the sheet of paper, and waved it in front of Pérez, who just smiled.

"I know what you said to me, I just wish you had not been so right. This damn suit is getting expensive. When do you think we'll get to trial?"

"The last time I checked with the court, we are scheduled to go next September 14. That's six weeks away, and I know we have been given the number one position, and I know that the lawsuit is not going to settle out of court, so we're next, and only a world disaster could cause us to lose our number one spot. So get ready, we are going to trial. And, by the way, just so you don't say I didn't tell you, we are probably going to be in trial for about a week, so you should expect to get another hefty bill after the trial is over. About half of what you have already been billed, so don't cry when you get it. You have been forewarned," Reynaldo told his client.

Chapter Twenty-four

With a short time left before the trial, Pérez and Reynaldo met every Saturday or Sunday to go over the facts of the case. They reviewed Pérez's testimony and talked about their witnesses. Reynaldo reviewed the file at least once a day. He needed to be entirely and thoroughly familiar with every pleading, letter, and deposition. One thing that Reynaldo learned early in his career was that he might not be smarter than opposing counsel, but he was not going to be out-prepared.

Finally, the scheduled Monday trial date was upon them. Reynaldo told his client to accompany him to court and had all the other witnesses on standby. To pick a jury he only needed his client. He told Pérez that the courthouse would be full of potential jurors that had been summoned to jury duty and that although he might know many of them personally, he should only greet them casually. Any familiarity could cause disqualification of the juror for service in his case.

"It's better to have twelve of your friends try your case than twelve strangers, so don't talk to them, just greet them. Later when the judge explains the procedure, they will understand why you did not stop to talk with them," Reynaldo told Pérez.

Reynaldo and his client walked into the courtroom and took their seats at the counsel table. Reynaldo put his briefcase and on the table and then began to look over the jury pool.

"I want you to make a mental note of the people that you know," he told his client. "I want to know who are your friends and who are your enemies, especially your enemies. If there's anyone out there that does not like you, I want you to tell me so I know how to question them."

There were ten cases set for trial that week. The Pérez case was at the top of the list. After twenty minutes the court bailiff announced the opening of court. He startled everyone as he shouted, "All rise. Oyez, Oyez, Oyez, the Honorable, the 184th District Court is now in session, the Honorable Carlos Zapata presiding. God bless this country, God bless this state, God bless this Honorable court. Please be seated."

There was a big shuffle of human movement as everyone took their chairs.

"Good morning ladies and gentlemen, and welcome to your 184th District Court," Judge Zapata smiled at the voters.

"I want to thank you for taking time from your busy schedules to perform your civic duty of serving as jurors," the judge said, addressing the prospective jurors. "Without your presence, these cases could not be heard. I know that you would rather not be here, but someone must perform this function. Someday, God forbid, when you have a matter that must be litigated you will be thankful that a jury will be around to help you settle your dispute. It isn't much, but at least you will get ten dollars per day and your meals.

"Now before we get started, let me take a moment to consult with the attorneys on the matter of the cases that we have on the docket. The first case is *Pérez v. Flores*. Mr. Reynaldo García, what announcement does the plaintiff make?"

Reynaldo and Cantu both rose to their feet and announced ready for trial.

"Is there any chance that this case will settle?" the judge asked.

"No your Honor, we have tried to settle this matter but could not reach an agreement," Reynaldo replied.

"Very well then you are number one in the docket, and you will pick a jury momentarily," Judge Zapata told them.

The judge inquired of the number two and three cases. The number two case had settled, and therefore all cases moved up a notch. The judge announced that they would pick jurors for the top three cases and told those involved in the other cases to report back the following Monday. The announcement was met with a low moan, as the attorneys and witnesses for the other cases shuffled out of the courtroom.

"There, now we can begin," the judge said. "There are one hundred ten of you potential jurors here this morning. What we are about to do, first, is find out which of you are qualified to be jurors. Then we will determine which of you may be disqualified because you know the parties or the attorneys to the degree that would compromise your views on the case. Those will most likely be disqualified."

The judge explained that to be legally qualified jurors needed to be at least twenty-one years of age, a registered voter, and be able to read and write the English language. The prospective jurors were also entitled to be excused from service on a jury if they were older than sixty-five, had custody of children under the age of ten, or were a full-time student. Eighteen jurors came forward and were questioned by the judge and were allowed to leave.

"Now, I know that there are those of you that have reasons, good reasons, why you need to be elsewhere. These are not legal reasons, and certainly not exemptions, but we will hear from you now," the judge said and asked anyone wishing to be excused to come forward. Another twenty-two were allowed to leave.

There were seventy persons left on the jury panel, from which thirty-six would be picked, twelve for each of the three juries. The judge asked them some general questions on their ability to be fair and impartial and listen to all the evidence before making a decision. No one indicated that they could not be fair.

"Now the attorneys will ask you some questions. Mr. Reynaldo García, who represents the plaintiff Juan Pérez, will address you first," Judge Zapata told the jury.

Reynaldo came to his feet. He carried a list of the jurors in one hand and a yellow legal pad in the other. He approached the bar that separated the audience from the counsels' tables, the jury box, and the judge's bench.

"Ladies and gentlemen, all we want are twelve people to sit in this jury box that can be fair. We want them to listen to the evidence in this case, and follow the law as it is explained by the judge. That seems simple enough, but unfortunately, it isn't that easy. For example, I heard the judge ask you a minute ago if any of you knew Mr. Mario Cantu or Mr. Larry Flores, and none of you answered his question. Now I know that some of you do know them. In fact, I have seen you talk with them in a manner that tells me, and any reasonable person, that you know each other very well. So please let's be honest, let's be fair. All we want are twelve people that can sit on the jury and be fair. Now let's see hands from those of you who know Mr. Cantu or Mr. Flores," Reynaldo smiled to the group, not wanting to offend anyone.

Five hands went up, and Reynaldo wrote their names down.

"There we go, that's being honest. Now let's talk," Reynaldo said and proceeded to question each of the five potential jurors at length and found that they could not be fair, as they felt either bound to help Cantu or Flores or else would feel uncomfortable to decide against them. Reynaldo challenged the jurors for cause, which meant the judge should excuse them without Reynaldo having to use one of his six peremptory strikes. The judge agreed with Reynaldo and excused them, thanking them for their service and their honesty.

Reynaldo continued to question the panel and found two more persons whom he had sued and who upon further questioning admitted to holding a grudge against him. One readily admitted to not being able to remain objective, the other agreed he had a bias but insisted that he could be fair and impartial. One was dismissed by the judge, the other allowed to remain, requiring Reynaldo to use one of his peremptory strikes.

As Reynaldo continued, others admitted to knowing Juan Pérez and having had disagreements with him. Some acknowledged their inability to be fair, some would not. Reynaldo took copious notes.

When Reynaldo finished, Mario took over and began questioning jurors, along the same lines as Reynaldo with the same results. Finally, the panel was reduced to fifty-seven potential jurors.

The remaining list was shuffled, and after each side eliminated six jurors, the first twelve names remaining on that list served on the jury. The judge allowed them some time to review the list carefully, and pick their strikes.

Reynaldo and his client went to a room where they could have privacy and went over their notes and the new list carefully. Reynaldo quickly picked out five "frenemies" who admitted a grudge but would not disqualify themselves and struck through their names. He asked Juan to review the list carefully, and Juan contributed one name, of a person that he had disliked all his life, and he was sure the feeling was mutual. Reynaldo drew a heavy pencil line through the name. That made six strikes. Reynaldo signed the list, and the two men returned to the courtroom. Reynaldo instructed Pérez to sit at the counsel table while he delivered the list to the district clerk. Moments later, Mario emerged from another room with his client and gave his list to the clerk.

"As your name is called please come forward and sit in the jury box," the deputy district clerk announced in a loud voice. The names were called, and Reynaldo made a note of the twelve chosen ones. Oftentimes it was necessary to talk to jurors after a verdict and question them on their behavior in deciding a case. In some cases, if the jury did not follow the instructions carefully, Reynaldo had been able to prove jury misconduct and get the verdict reversed, or a mistrial declared.

The jury included a Border Patrol agent, a telephone repairman, a pharmacist, two school teachers, a nurse, and the rest nondescript people that Reynaldo did not know. He remembered that in his early trials he seemed to know everyone on the jury panels. These days he was lucky if he recognized one or two of the jurors.

"Ladies and gentlemen you are the jury in the *Pérez v. Flores* lawsuit. Please stand," Judge Zapata said and he proceeded to swear the jurors in. He then advised them not to discuss the case with anyone, including their spouses, and not to talk with any of the attorneys or the parties.

"Listen to the evidence carefully, and when instructed to answer the questions propounded by the court, return a verdict based only on evidence heard from the witness stand, or otherwise admitted by the judge, and not consider any other information," the judge continued.

Having finished his admonition, the judge dismissed them until one o'clock that afternoon when the trial was to get underway. The jury filed out of the courtroom.

"Mr. García and Mr. Cantu, we will start at once. Get all your witnesses ready and on standby. I don't want any unnecessary delays. Court is recessed until one o'clock," the judge announced as he stood up and went into his chambers.

"All rise," the bailiff shouted.

Chapter Twenty-five

In order to prove that his client was entitled to the two hundred acres, Reynaldo had to prove that Pérez was the owner of record. He had to establish that fact by the totality of the evidence. Once Reynaldo was able to accomplish that, then the burden shifted to the defendant to prove why his title was superior to that of Pérez.

The defendant needed to show that Pérez had lost the title to the property, even though he was record owner, because Flores had complied with all the requirements of the ten-year statute of limitation in acquiring title to the property by adverse possession. After both parties presented their evidence, the jury was asked to answer several questions called special issues and based on the answers to these, the judge rendered judgment in the case.

Since Pérez had the burden of proof, that meant that Reynaldo presented his case first by calling and examining all his witnesses. Then Mario presented his case on behalf of Flores, and Reynaldo had the opportunity to rebut Flores' evidence.

In a typical case, Reynaldo would have started with Pérez or the surveyor and then continued with his remaining witnesses, after which he would rest his case. In this trial, Reynaldo had a special plan of attack that he hoped would disrupt Mario's strategy and upset Flores for the rest of the week.

"Well we are now ready to commence, you may call your first witness Mr. García," Judge Zapata announced.

"The plaintiff calls Larry Flores as an adverse witness," Reynaldo announced, to the surprise of everyone in the courtroom.

Mario and Flores were both visibly shaken. Reynaldo had astonished them and thrown them off balance. For the remainder of the trial Flores and his attorney were unable to regain their footing. Mario explained to Flores that he had to get on the stand and testify. Flores walked across the courtroom toward the witness stand confused and reluctant and was interrupted by the district clerk.

"Excuse me, I have to swear you in first," the clerk blurted excitedly. Flores stopped abruptly, looked at Mario and then at the judge totally confused, not knowing what to do, nor where to do it. The jury giggled at the scene.

Finally, Flores took his place on the witness stand, and Reynaldo went to work. Flores was wearing a white shirt and tie. The tie was too short for his enormous stomach, and the shirt was so small that the material tore at the buttons. Flores was perspiring profusely.

Reynaldo began by going over the details of the purchase of the ranch from Minerva Pérez García, then honed in on the specifics of his supposed adverse possession.

"What did you do on the land for the eleven years you owned it?"

"I ranched on it, and hunted on it."

"Did you have cattle on it all the time?"

"I rotated the cattle from pasture to pasture, so the cattle were only there about three or four months out of the year."

"Did you do anything else with the land?"

"Well, we fixed the fences, and sometimes I would have the cowboys cut brush?"

"Mr. Flores, did you ever tell anyone that you were claiming the extra two hundred acres as your own?"

"No, no, no, I never told anyone, " Flores answered nervously.

"You didn't tell your cowboys, your tenants or even tell your wife and children that you were claiming the extra two hundred acres?"

"No sir, I did not."

Reynaldo kept hammering away, and Flores got more and more nervous. Finally, Flores broke down.

"Your Honor, I don't feel good. I have a pain in my chest, I need a rest, Your Honor. I'm not used to this. I am very nervous. If I could just have a rest, Your Honor," Flores pleaded in a weak cry.

"Very well, we'll take a brief recess. Ladies and gentlemen of the jury, come back in ten minutes. We have a lot of work to do, so we're not taking long breaks. Be back in ten minutes. Don't talk to anyone about the case. Do not discuss the case with anyone."

"All rise," the bailiff yelled out. Everyone came to their feet, as the judge exited the courtroom. Flores stepped down from the witness stand as the jury filed out of the courtroom. Mario comforted him and gave him a drink of water.

Reynaldo gloated at how well his strategy was working. Pérez just smiled and shook his head. He too could see the effect of the surprise attack.

After fifteen minutes, the Court reconvened, and Reynaldo continued grilling Flores.

"Look at these mortgages that you made at the State Bank and Trust her in Laredo. Did you include the two hundred acres in the mortgages?"

"No sir, I did not."

"Did you pay taxes on the property?"

"No sir, I did not."

"Did you ever tell Juan Pérez that you were claiming two hundred of his acres, whether he liked it or not?"

"No sir, I did not."

"Why not?"

"Well if I had told Juan Pérez he would have taken it by force, or else he would have sued me immediately?"

"Well then tell all these fine people here on the jury, how do you think this property is yours now?"

"I have possessed it for eleven years now. It has been within my fences for eleven years, and that's why it's mine."

"And you knew immediately after you bought the property that you got two hundred more acres than you paid for because you had the property surveyed immediately. Isn't that a fact?"

"Yes sir, I knew right away."

Reynaldo questioned him for the remainder of the afternoon and was not through with Flores when the court adjourned for the day.

"Ladies and gentlemen, we are going to adjourn," Judge Zapata announced. "Now in the old days, I would have sent you to a hotel and sequestered you from your friends and family. I think we have grown out of that, so I am going to let you go home, but I warn you not to discuss this case with anyone, not even members of your immediate family. That is the law, and I do not want you interfered with by anybody. If anyone tries to talk with you, I want to know it immediately. Do not read newspaper accounts of the trial, and if you hear something on TV or on the radio about this case, turn the set off immediately. That is all. I expect you to be here at eight thirty in the morning."

"All rise," the bailiff shouted out.

The attorneys gathered their materials slowly, chatted with their clients, and eventually made their way out of the courtroom. Reynaldo told Pérez to go on home and be at his office at eight.

Being early risers, Reynaldo and Pérez met at the office at seven thirty and discussed the technicalities of the trial while they drank coffee in the library. They were both in an extremely good mood.

"Things are going good now Juan, but remember you still have to get on the stand. Mario will try to make picadillo out of you too. I don't mean to scare you, but we have to expect some opposition."

They chatted as Reynaldo filled his briefcase for the short walk to the courthouse.

By fifteen minutes after eight, all the jurors were sitting in the jury box. Reynaldo and his client walked in, and Reynaldo insisted on looking at each of the jurors in the eye. The responses he got were favorable. Each of the jurors looked straight back at him, and most of them smiled at him.

"Things are going well," he thought to himself.

Reynaldo resumed with the skewering of Flores at eight forty-five. Flores had changed to a sports shirt. He could not continue with the facade of the business attire, but he was still perspiring, wringing his hands, and acting very nervous.

"Mr. Flores, I'll remind you that you are still under oath. Did you built the fence that encloses the two hundred acres in question in the trial?"

"No sir I did not."

"Do you know who built it and when?"

"No sir I do not."

"And the two hundred acres are definitely not in the deed you got from Minerva Pérez García?"

"Well, I got a deed to the Minerva García Ranch ten miles east of Laredo in Webb County, Texas. That's all I know," Flores replied. He appeared more relaxed this second day and seemed to be ready to go on the offensive.

"Well let's look at the deed," Reynaldo resumed his questioning. "Doesn't it say two thousand two hundred acres? It doesn't say two thousand four hundred acres does it?"

"It does not say two thousand four hundred," Flores responded as if deciding not to match wits with the attorney after all.

"I believe you stated that you saw Juan Pérez repairing the division fence, on many occasions, is that correct?"

"Occasionally when I went out there, he was fixing it."

After two hours of intensive questioning, Reynaldo decided to wrap up his examination of Flores.

"Now, in summary, Mr. Flores, you did not exercise any control over the two hundred acres, you did not pay taxes on them, you did not mortgage them, and you did not tell anyone you were claiming them as your own. You were just hiding behind the log, hoping that someday maybe they would become yours. Isn't that so?"

"Yes, I guess you are right, I was hiding behind the log."

"I'll pass the witness," Reynaldo said to Mario, who set out to rehabilitate his client for the remainder of the day, but the damage was done.

On the third day of the trial, Reynaldo called Frank Santos an attorney whom he had employed as an expert witness. Santos had purchased an abstract of title, a complete compilation of all documents ever filed for the record concerning or touching on the Juan Pérez ranch. The abstract had cost $10,000 and was nine hundred pages long. A fact that made Pérez wince.

Santos had a particular skill of examining titles and an excellent reputation for being very competent in his field. His opinion was widely respected by the entire bar, even Mario.

Santos explained the history of the property, which began in 1755 when the Spanish viceroy had the entire area surveyed, parceled out and granted to settlers. The first grantee from the King of Spain was one Miguel Rodríguez, who was granted about fifty thousand acres. The property stayed in the Rodríguez family for nearly eighty years. After exchanging hands numerous times, Pérez's mother inherited four thousand four hundred acres, which she left to her children, Juan Pérez and Minerva Pérez García. Santos went over the abstract, detail by meticulous detail, finally identifying the two hundred acres, and concluding that Pérez was the record owner of the land. Santos, moreover, testified that Pérez had paid property taxes on the two hundred acres since he inherited the land. As proof, Santos pointed to tax records for corroboration.

Santos' testimony was so precise and skillful, that Mario, in a sage move, declined to cross-examine him. It was an axiom in the legal trade, "if you don't know what the witness is going to say, or if the witness is brilliant, leave him alone, don't ask him questions, because he will probably hurt you."

The fourth day, Reynaldo called Alfredo Treviño, who had surveyed the property in dispute. Pérez had finally agreed to pay for a survey. Treviño had gone over and rechecked the Flores survey that had been made eleven years prior and confirmed that the 200 acres in question had been erroneously included. His own survey, Treviño told the jury, confirmed that the two hundred acres belonged to Pérez.

With the Treviño and Santos testimony, there was no question on the record ownership, location and amount of acreage in dispute.

Treviño was fair game, surveying is an inaccurate science, and Mario questioned him most of the day, trying to trip him up and discredit his ability in surveying and making conclusions from his survey calculations. Treviño had been a surveyor for thirty years and had testified many times. There was no danger that Mario could confuse him or rattle him. He plodded along and did not vary his testimony. Try as he might, Mario was unable to impeach his testimony. After persisting for hour after hour, the judge finally told him to move to someone or something else.

Reynaldo spent the fifth day with several shorter less critical witnesses. He called Minerva Pérez García to explain that she had not intended to sell Flores the two hundred acres that belonged to her brother, but only what she had inherited. And that she had never wanted to nor intentionally possessed any property adversely against her brother. It was evident of course that she had not, but Reynaldo had to present this testimony to the jury. He could leave no stone unturned. He had to eliminate all doubt in the jurors' minds.

Reynaldo summed up the day with adjacent landowners who dealt with Flores, and Flores' tenants, to prove that Flores had never communicated to them that he was claiming an additional two hundred acres.

Reynaldo had been very thorough and efficient with time. But he could not finish until his client testified. It was late

Friday afternoon, and nobody cared to work on Saturday, certainly not the jurors. Nothing would be gained by working on Saturday. The judge decided to resume testimony on Monday, an announcement that greatly displeased other attorneys that were scheduled to begin their trial on that date.

Chapter Twenty-six

On Monday morning Reynaldo called Pérez to the stand. He had to establish the facts of non-consent, no knowledge, no clear notice, no adversity, and no hostility toward him by Flores.

Reynaldo learned early on as an attorney that the record, which consisted of the transcribed objections, questions, and answers of the entire trial, and, all of the documents filed in the lawsuit must cover all parts and issues of his case, even at the expense of being redundant. Many times in reviewing the statement of facts in other cases he could see that sometimes he asked the same questions dozens of times. At first, he thought of himself as being boring, and repetitive, but as time went on, he realized that the redundancy was necessary. To ensure that no stone was left unturned, and equally important that on appeal, the appellate judges had plenty of testimony to establish a particular fact, despite any other evidence in conflict with the truth.

Paul Banks, the senior partner at the law firm where Reynaldo had started his legal career had explained the concept to him.

"The Appellate Court will not overturn a verdict if there is a great preponderance of evidence to support the verdict. In other words, the Appellate Court is not going to replace the jury. It is only when there is an absence of evidence, just absolutely none, not even a whisper, that the appellate judges will reverse because of no evidence. In such a case they will substitute their judgment for the ruling that the trial court should have rendered. That's called reversed and rendered. If there is some evidence

to support the lower court's decision, ninety-nine times out of a hundred the Appellate Court will leave the verdict alone. It is only when there is very little evidence to support the verdict, and all the weight of the evidence is against the judgment, and it is apparent that the jury got carried away with some emotion like passion or anger, and disregarded all the proper evidence, then the Appellate Court will reverse the judgment and order a new trial. That's called reversed and remanded.

"And let me tell you something Ray, it is critical that you try and win in the trial court because having to appeal, is like trying to climb up and an icy hill at about a ten-degree incline. It is hard. The Appellate Courts are very reluctant to disturb what a jury of twelve people agreed to, and to which the trial judge also decided. You see if the judge did not agree with the jury, and if the judge also thought that there was absolutely no evidence, or that the jury had gotten away and disregarded the preponderance of the evidence, the judge would and should grant a judgment or a directed verdict, notwithstanding the jury's finding.

"But when an appellate judge sees the jury's findings, and the trial judge didn't do anything about it, then the appellate judge thinks right away that twelve voters and a judge, who usually is a powerful person, all decided a certain way, then why should he go around acting like God and deciding things different. You know what I mean?" Banks asked him.

Reynaldo knew what he meant, although it took a while before he understood completely and exactly what Banks had described. So it was that Reynaldo proceeded to present as much good, competent evidence as he could find, and that included grilling Pérez until noon.

After lunch, Mario took over and cross-examined Pérez who was no intellectual and could not match wits with Mario. Fortunately, he did not try. Mario tried to mix him up and get him to change his story, but Pérez's naiveté and sincerity triumphed every time, and the jury quickly took a liking to the old cowboy.

It appeared that the jury felt uncomfortable when Mario questioned him too fiercely.

The judge called a recess at three o'clock, and Pérez let on to Reynaldo that he was very nervous, and scared.

"I'll be damned glad when this shit is over, I am really nervous. I feel the hot burning blood in my neck, in my head, and in my chest. You know I remember a story about an old cowboy in Duval County, who had a problem with a city pansy like Larry Flores. He just got out the old forty-five thumb buster, got in his pickup, drove over to the pansy's house, and confronted him, and told him if he didn't move the fence, he was going to kill him. Ole Pansy Whistlebritches, hell, he moved the fence the next day, cause he knew if he didn't he was gonna be a dead man. That's what I should'a done with this damn sonofabitch Flores. Of course, with my luck, hell I'd go to the pen for sure. For a hunnert years. Hell, I sure wish this was over now," Pérez lamented.

"Listen, Juan, you are doing fine, don't crater on me now," Reynaldo told his client. "Let me assure you that you are doing just fine. Just relax. In a couple of hours, we'll be drinking some cold beer. Just relax, you'll see, everything is turning out just fine. Boy if I had to bet money, I would say, Mr. Pérez, that this cake is about ready and it's ours, so don't crater on me, just a little more time."

The next hour was unproductive, Pérez finished testifying about four thirty, and Mario used only the remaining two hours for rebuttal testimony. Most of the evidence had already been brought out in direct and cross-examination, leaving very little to be accomplished in rebuttal witness testimony.

At seven o'clock the judge dismissed the jury for the day, explaining the procedures that they were to follow.

"Ladies and gentlemen of the jury, this trial is almost concluded. I am going to allow you to go home now, and return at nine o'clock tomorrow morning. Right now the attorneys and I are going to continue working on what is known as the jury charge which is a small packet of papers that will explain to you the job of reaching a verdict. The jury charge will be addressed to you, and it will give you instructions on what to do. It will give you the applicable law in this case, and then it will give you several questions that you must answer. In this case, one or both of the parties have elected to have their case tried by a jury instead of the judge. That means that the jury, and not the judge, must go through the facts, decide who is telling the truth and who is not, and decide which witness and which testimony is to be given more weight. All that will be explained to you in the morning in much more detail, I just wanted to give you an idea of what you will be doing tomorrow. For now, you are dismissed, and we'll see you bright eyed and bushy tailed in the morning," Judge Zapata concluded as the jury laughed, and he rose and left for his chambers.

"All rise," the bailiff again shouted.

Chapter
Twenty-seven

Each of the attorneys advised their clients that they still had work to do on the charge and the judge instructed them to go home and get some rest since the trial would not resume until morning. Reynaldo and Mario walked into the judge's chambers where they found a relaxed Judge Zapata who had removed his robe.

"Come in, come in you pricks," he was tired and tried to be funny. "Well, we got another one under our belt. I just wonder how many trials we are all going to try in how many years?"

Judge Zapata looked out his office window as the bailiff poured all three a whiskey on ice. The two attorneys sat at chairs in front of the judge's desk.

"OK, let's get started," the judge suddenly got back to the business and handed them his draft of the charge to the jury. "Rey do you have your issues ready? Mario where are yours?"

The attorneys handed over their suggested additions to the charge.

"Mr. Leon, you better get in close, because we have to have all this proceeding on the record, in case I screw up," the judge motioned to the court reporter. "One of these gentlemen might want to bare my ass to the Appellate Court, so get in close."

The judge grinned to the court reporter as he sipped on his whiskey.

"OK. Rey you are the plaintiff, so let's start on your questions. Go one by one, and tell me why you think the question belongs in the charge. Mario when I'm through with him, you tell me why you think it should not be in the charge. All right let's go, and let's try to hurry a little, it's late, and I miss momma."

For the next hour and a half, the three worked feverishly giving and taking, each performing to the best of his talent. The offer, the objection, the dictation, the transcription, the ruling, the preservation of error on the record, the final formulation of the lengthy document called the jury charge.

Reynaldo and Mario left the courthouse exhausted. They bid each other good night and headed to their respective homes.

The following morning, Reynaldo and his client once again met for coffee in the library at the law office. They sipped and chatted quietly. The battle was over, all that was missing was the declaration of who had won. Reynaldo was very tired, but still could not let his guard down. He still had to give a final argument or summation. He had practiced his presentation over breakfast with Mari Lou. Every lawyer has his own style for closing arguments. Some memorize everything, others read everything, and still, others ad-lib or wing it, using a small list of salient points in logical order as reminders. Reynaldo and Mario employed the latter style. Each spewed a multitude of thoughts, all seeming to fall into perfect logical order.

As the hour neared, Reynaldo began to stuff his large briefcase with the entire file.

"Why do you take the whole file, the trial is over, and all you need is the charge?" Pérez asked.

"I need the whole file because if I want to look up a minor point, I want to be able to look it up and find the answer. Otherwise, the curiosity will distract me from the rest of my summation," Reynaldo explained.

As the two men walked into the courtroom, they noticed the jury box was almost full. Reynaldo took his eye stare test, and the result was positive. The two sat at the counsel table. In a short while, Mario and Flores took their seats to wait for the judge to make his entrance.

Reynaldo and Mario, carefully went over their notes, oblivious to the people around them. The bailiff suddenly interrupted their thought process.

"All counsel in the judge's chambers," he shouted.

Reynaldo and Mario quickly walked into chambers.

"Good morning Rey, Mario, how are you two this morning?" Judge Zapata greeted the two attorneys.

"Fine your honor," they both answered at the same time.

"We're going on the record now," the judge said, motioning to the court reporter.

"Gentlemen, we worked until midnight on the jury charge, and it is ready. I am delivering a copy of it to each of you now. I want you to read it carefully, and in fifteen minutes I want you to begin voicing your objections to the charge into the record. Mr. Leon here is ready to take your dictation all morning.

"Now I worked extra hard on this charge, and I am not going to change it no matter what. I know that sometimes, we make changes to the jury charge, after hearing objections. Well, that is not the case today. I have gone over it with a fine tooth comb, and I am very satisfied with it, and if you don't like it then just dictate your objection, and if your complaint is valid, the boys in the ivory tower, at the appellate level will have a shot at either agreeing with you or disagreeing with you. But there will be no changes.

"Now please start reading. I am leaving for some coffee, and I will return in thirty minutes. By that time I expect the plaintiff to be finished or close to finished dictating objections, and then the defendant will follow," Judge Zapata said and walked out.

Reynaldo was surprised to hear Judge Zapata be so forceful. Usually, he was scared of his shadow, and would not dare go to the jury without changing the jury charge three or four times.

After the judge left, the two lawyers read in silence. The court reporter interrupted them to let them know that the judge had just returned from a judge's conference where they had been given an example of a charge in a land case just like the one they were trying. Reynaldo now understood the judge's uncharacteristic degree of confidence in his charge.

After several minutes, and two very close examinations, Reynaldo began his objections.

"There is no evidence, or there is insufficient evidence to submit issue number two to the jury. As a matter of law, this court should grant a directed verdict. The evidence clearly shows that there is no fact question as a matter of law. There is not even a scintilla of evidence, not a shred of evidence. As a matter of law, without the necessity of a jury, this court should rule."

Reynaldo's objections went on for several minutes, at which time Reynaldo yielded to Mario who likewise went through a similar soliloquy.

When Mario was finished, Mr. Leon broke the silence.

"May I ask why you make so many objections to a charge that basically you two prepared?"

"Because if we do not object we waive all objection, and if we have to go on appeal, the Appellate Court will not let us complain of the District Court's error if we have not preserved error by dictating objections," Reynaldo explained.

The judge had returned as Reynaldo was finishing his dictation, and sat in a back seat, and watched the two lawyers work. He marveled at their ability. They were like gladiators, jet fighters, heavyweights. He knew, of course, that he was not one and would never become one.

Finally, the objections were finished. The judge told the attorneys to wait for him in the courtroom.

"All rise!" the bailiff once again roared a few minutes later. "The 184th District Court for Webb County is now in session, the Honorable Carlos Zapata presiding. God Bless this country,

God bless this state, God bless this Honorable court. Please be seated."

"Good morning ladies and gentlemen. I am sorry we are a little late but we were preparing this," Judge Zapata began, showing the jury charge to the jury. "You should all have a copy now, and I want you to read along with me as I go over every bit of it for you."

"Ladies and Gentlemen of the Jury: This case is submitted to you by asking questions about the facts, which you must decide from the evidence you have heard in this trial. You are the sole judges of the credibility of the witnesses and the weight to be given their testimony, but in matters of law, you must be governed by the instructions in this charge.

"In discharging your responsibility as the jury, you will observe all the instructions which have previously been given to you. I shall now give you additional guidelines which you should carefully and strictly follow during your deliberations," Judge Zapata read the jury charge and then listed the instructions the jury was to follow.

1. Do not let bias, prejudice nor sympathy play any part in your discussions.

2. In arriving at your answers, consider only the evidence introduced here under oath, such as exhibits, if any, as have been presented for your consideration under the rulings of the Court. That is, what you have seen and heard in this courtroom, together with the law as given you by the Court. In your deliberations, you will not consider or discuss anything that is not represented by the evidence in this case.

3. Since every answer that is required by the charge is important, no juror should state or consider that any required answer is not necessary.

4. You must not decide who you think should win, and then try to answer the questions accordingly. Just answer the

questions, and do not concern yourselves with the effect of your answers.

5. You will not decide the answer to a question by lot or by drawing straws, or by any other method of chance. Do not return a quotient verdict, which means that the jurors agree to abide by the result to be reached by adding together each juror's figures and dividing by the number of jurors to get an average. Do not do any trading on your answers; that is, one juror should not agree to answer a specific question one way if others will decide to answer another question another way.

6. You may render your verdict upon the vote of ten or more members of the jury. The same ten or more of you must agree upon all of the answers made and to the entire verdict. You will not, therefore, enter into an agreement to be bound by a majority or any other vote of fewer than ten jurors. If the verdict and all of the answers therein are reached by unanimous agreement, the presiding juror shall sign the judgment for the entire jury. If any juror disagrees as to any answer made by the verdict, those jurors who agree to all findings shall each sign the judgment.

"These instructions are given to you because your conduct is subject to review the same way as that of the witnesses, parties, attorneys, and the judge. If it should be found that you have disregarded any of these instructions, it will be considered as jury misconduct, and it may require another trial by another jury; then, all of our time will have been wasted.

"The presiding juror or any other juror who observes a violation of the Court's instructions must immediately warn the one who is violating the same and caution the juror not to do so again.

"The questions usually, though not always, begin with the phrase 'Do you find from a preponderance of the evidence' that a particular fact, act, omission or transaction took place. The preponderance of the evidence means the high weight and degree of credible testimony or evidence introduced before you and admitted in evidence in this case.

"The following are the definitions that you will use in answering the questions, which are submitted to you, which are also called special issues. This case is presented to you on a special verdict, which means you answer questions instead of rendering a general opinion, as to which party should win.

"A deed is a document which conveys, transfers, sells or grants the title to real estate or property.

"Record title owner is that person, company or entity who appears to hold the title to the real estate in question as contained in the records at the courthouse.

"The term peaceable possession is such possession of real estate that is continuous and uninterrupted by an adverse lawsuit to recover the same real estate.

"Adverse possession is an actual and peaceable appropriation of the land or real estate, commenced and continued under a claim of right inconsistent with and hostile to the claim of another. The use and enjoyment of the land is necessary to make its possession adverse under our limitation statutes mainly only that to which the property is adaptable and capable of being used.

"By claim of right is meant an intention to claim the land as one's own.

"Hostile means a holding out with intent to claim the land as one's own to the exclusion of all others. You are instructed that by the term hostile is meant an occupancy of the premises under a holding by the possessor as owner, and therefore against all other claimants of the land.

"Paying taxes thereon means paying from year to year as the taxes accrue and before they are delinquent, and includes all taxes assessed against the land.

"Mortgaging land means conveying or transferring the land to a party to secure or guarantee or collateralize the loan of money."

Following the explanation of the definitions, Judge Zapata read the special issues to the jury.

"You will find the questions or special issues which you must answer following this charge and the above definitions and instructions," said the judge, reading the special issues slowly and deliberately, after which the judge called a short recess.

Chapter Twenty-eight

The judge knew that he was about to send the jury to consider the case and called a recess to let everyone have one final bathroom break before they began deliberations. Through experience, Judge Zapata knew that if he controlled the bathroom visit, it would be over in ten minutes, but if he let the jurors go to the jury room without the bathroom visit, they would take an hour to finish their break and finally begin deliberations. By the end of the ten-minute break, the jurors were back in the jury box, the attorneys and clients at their tables, and the judge came back into the room.

"All rise," the bailiff shouted, and the judge sat at the bench.

"Just a few more instructions, and then you may retire to the jury room," the judge told the jury.

"After you retire to the jury room, you will select one of your own as Presiding Juror. The first thing the Presiding Juror will do is to have this complete charge read aloud and, then, you will deliberate upon your answers to the questions asked. The Presiding Juror will preside during your deliberations and see to it that your proceedings are conducted in an orderly manner and following the instructions in this charge. He or she will write and hand to the bailiff any communication concerning the case which the jury desires to have delivered to the judge. To vote on the questions write your answers to the questions in the spaces provided and

certify the jury's verdict in the area provided for the presiding juror's signature. If needed, obtain the signatures of all the jurors who agree with the decision if your verdict is less than unanimous.

"After you have retired to consider your verdict, no one has any authority to communicate with you, except the bailiff of this Court. You should not discuss the case with anyone not even with other members of the jury unless all of you are present and assembled in the jury room. Should anyone attempt to talk to you about the case before the verdict is returned, whether at the Courthouse, at your home, or elsewhere, please inform me as soon as possible.

"When you are ready you will advise the bailiff at the door of the jury room that you have reached a verdict.

"Signed, Carlos Zapata, Judge of the 184th District Court," the judge finished reading the long charge.

"Now the attorneys will address you in their final summation. Mr. Reynaldo García represents the plaintiff Juan Pérez, and bearing the burden of proof will commence the argument and rebut any argument or summation by Mr. Mario Cantu who represents the defendant Larry Flores. Mr. García, you may commence."

Reynaldo slowly began going over all of the testimony, emphasizing the lack of adverse possession by Flores. Reynaldo liked final jury arguments. He often referred to attorneys as frustrated actors who loved to hear themselves talk to a group of people. Reynaldo frequently joked to Mari Lou that his argument consisted of gold and silver ribbon and lace flowing from his mouth and silver tongue, occasionally accented by chorizo and tacos. He emphasized the law, of course, but he really hammered away at the "hiding behind the log" character of the possession.

"How can you have 'claim of right' or 'hostility' as those terms are defined in this charge, if the defendant never told anyone that he was claiming the land, never paid taxes on it, and never mortgaged the property. You can't have a claim of right or hostility if you don't even tell your wife about it," Reynaldo said, slapping the charge into his free hand as he argued.

After Reynaldo's opening statement, Mario emphasized, the holding of the land within boundary fences and use in grazing cattle, hunting, the lapse of time, and general appropriation. He knew that even if he did not have all the requisite elements, the jury could find the existence of a fact anyway, disregarding the evidence, and if they did Reynaldo would have a hell of a job appealing an adverse verdict. All was fair. What counted was winning, after that whoever lost had a horrible uphill battle.

After Mario finished, Reynaldo having the burden of proof as the plaintiff was allowed to close the argument. Mario could not argue again. Reynaldo went over his prior case and attacked Mario's points. He summarized the evidence, and then went over each of the questions and told them why he wanted them answered his way. Finally, he asked them to find in favor of his client.

"If ever a case pleads, and begs for justice, it is this one. How can a person be allowed to keep someone else's property for ten years and claim it as his own? That is stealing, and you know it," Reynaldo said in closing.

Mario jumped to his feet.

"Objection, your honor. Keeping the property for ten years, and claiming it is perfectly legal, and counsel's characterization is extremely unfair and prejudicial. The defendant Larry Flores moves for a mistrial," Mario shouted as he rose in anger.

"The motion for mistrial is denied. Counsel, keep your argument proper. An old veteran like you knows better. Please don't stray from the rules. Continue your argument," Judge Zapata told Reynaldo to Mario's displeasure.

Reynaldo continued his closing statement.

"You told me a week ago, that you knew that you could render a fair and impartial verdict based on the evidence presented from the witness stand. You have heard it all, so go do your job, go do what you told me you would do, go answer these questions fairly and impartially. Go do justice. I thank you for your very kind attention," Reynaldo said in closing.

"Ladies and gentlemen, like counsel said, go do your job. Take the jury charges, and file on out to the jury room. If you need anything, please advise the bailiff, he will be sitting just outside your door. Normally I would let you go out for lunch, but we have been here long enough, and I don't care to delay this matter any longer, so I have sent out for box lunches, and you will get these in about an hour," the judge told the jury. "Please let me know through the bailiff if you have any questions. I can tell you that I know you will probably have to work hard, it is not going to be fast nor pleasant. I can also tell you that the system cannot work without you and that everyone appreciates your help. Please go do your job."

The jury stood and filed out as the bailiff once again asked everyone to rise.

Like most attorneys, Reynaldo was snowed under with work. He preferred to be at the office trying to catch up. In reality, he would rather be fishing on a quiet ranch stock tank, with a case of beer, and a rack of ribs sizzling on a grill.

His conscience never let him take the fishing trip. Instead, he plodded along at the office trying to catch up with work that just kept pouring in. The unfortunate thing was that a lot of it would never be paid. He knew one-third of his work went unpaid. He cursed himself for not being stricter with his clients and demanding money in advance. He could not bring himself to do it, feeling sorry for the misfortune that most suffered. He concluded that litigation was out of the reach of most, economi-cally, and that somehow he had a duty to make justice accessible to all. He was thankful to God for his health and affluence.

When he waited for a jury, he usually stayed at the courthouse. Working on other case files occupied part of his time, but the anticlimax of a grueling trial sometimes prohibited concentration on a new client.

Reynaldo ambled through the courtroom, then to the staff offices where a bored bureaucrat was always available for idle conversation. Then he wandered out to the hall and back into the courtroom, chatting with whoever was available. He talked to Pérez and his family.

Around noon, Reynaldo and the Pérez family walked to the Plaza Hotel for lunch. The talk was still about the trial, but now they ventured off to other topics. They hurried the meal, and rushed back to the courthouse, not knowing that the jury verdict was still hours away.

Reynaldo walked over to Mario, and the two men talked about their colleagues, certain controversial cases, and politics.

"I was talking to Bernardo the other day, and he told me that he is planning one of the biggest July 4th parties that he has ever had," Mario told Reynaldo. "He plans on inviting the President of the United States. Of course, he doesn't expect him to come, but he is inviting everyone that is anyone. That guy really gets carried away with politics. I thought I was bad, but he really is really consumed by it."

They continued talking, for a long while and, finally, they separated and walked around killing time.

Reynaldo called his office every hour. He was starting to formulate a plan of attack on all the ignored work that was stacked up on his desk and other tables at the office.

Finally, it came time for supper, and he turned down an invitation from the Pérez family, and told them to go without him. They were back in twenty minutes.

At about nine o'clock three loud bangs were heard on the jury room door. Finally, they had a verdict. Reynaldo was confident that things would turn out all right, but then again, as he had repeatedly advised Pérez, it was impossible to predict what a jury would do.

The judge was advised, and he took the bench and asked to bring the jury back into the courtroom. When they were back in the jury box, he asked if they had a verdict and the Presiding Juror answered in the affirmative.

"Then just give the verdict to Miss Garza there, and she will read it. Just read the special issues and the answers, there is no need to reread the whole charge," Judge Zapata instructed the clerk.

"Yes sir, of course," Miss Garza arranged the tight dress on her flabby body, adjusted her glasses, cleared her throat, and began to speak in a loud high pitched voice.

SPECIAL ISSUE NO. 1

Do you find from a preponderance of the evidence that Juan Pérez is the record owner of the two hundred acres in question?

Answer: We do.

SPECIAL ISSUE NO. 2

Do you find from a preponderance of the evidence that the deed from Minerva García to Larry Flores did not include the two hundred acres in question?

Answer: We do.

SPECIAL ISSUE NO. 3

Do you find from the preponderance of the evidence that Larry Flores never paid property ad valorem taxes on the two hundred acres in question?

Answer: We do.

SPECIAL ISSUE NO. 4

Do you find from a preponderance of the evidence that Larry Flores, while having an opportunity to do so, never included the subject two hundred acres, in mortgages to his bank?

Answer: We do.

SPECIAL ISSUE NO. 5

Do you find from a preponderance of the evidence that Larry Flores had continuous possession and enjoyment of the two hundred acres in dispute not interrupted by an adverse lawsuit for ten years or more prior to the filing of this lawsuit?

Answer: We do not

SPECIAL ISSUE NO. 6

Do you find from a preponderance of the evidence that Larry Flores actually and visibly appropriated the land in dispute for ten years or more prior to the filing of this suit?

Answer: We do not.

SPECIAL ISSUE NO. 7

Do you find from a preponderance of the evidence that such actual and visible appropriation commenced and continued with the intentions of claiming the land for himself for ten years or more prior to the filing of this suit?

Answer: We do not.

SPECIAL ISSUE NO. 8

Do you find from a preponderance of the evidence that appropriation of the land in dispute, if any you have found, by Larry Flores, was of such a character as to indicate unmistakably an assertion of a claim of exclusive ownership?

Answer: We do not.

SPECIAL ISSUE NO. 9

Do you find from a preponderance of the evidence, that the two hundred acres in dispute, were enclosed within the fences of the Larry Flores ranch?

Answer: We do.

SPECIAL ISSUE NO. 10

Do you find from a preponderance of the evidence that the enclosure of the two hundred acres within the fences of the Larry Flores Ranch was the result of a casual, incidental or accidental fencing?

Answer: We do.

SPECIAL ISSUE NO. 11

Do you find from a preponderance of the evidence in this case that Larry Flores, whether in person or through a tenant

or tenants, or partly in person, and partly through a tenant or tenants, held exclusive, peaceable and adverse possession of the land in dispute in this suit? That he cultivated, used or enjoyed the same for ten years or longer than ten years before the filing of this lawsuit?

Answer: We do not.

SPECIAL ISSUE NO. 12

Do you find from a preponderance of the evidence in this case that Juan Pérez knew that the defendant Larry Flores was claiming the land in controversy in this suit adverse to Juan Pérez?

Answer: We do not.

SPECIAL ISSUE NO. 13

Do you find from a preponderance of the evidence in this case that the defendant Larry Flores, asserted adverse possession, if any, to the two hundred acres in dispute, against Juan Pérez such as was of such unequivocal notoriety and hostility, and adversity that Juan Pérez would be presumed to have notice of such adverse claim and possession?

Answer: We do not.

Reynaldo had the burden of proving that Pérez was the record owner of the two hundred acres, which he did through Frank Santos the attorney, and through Alfredo Treviño, the surveyor. After that the burden shifted to Mario to prove from a preponderance of the evidence that Flores had possessed the property adversely, meeting the requirements of the statute, for ten years or more. Most of the special issues were submitted by Mario, and he had expected a finding in his favor. Several of the issues were shades of others already offered, thus giving him a double bite at the apple or a second opportunity to get a favorable finding. Reynaldo had objected to the double submission, but Judge Zapata had refused to change the charge as he had prepared it. The objection had been unnecessary, however, as all of the issues had been answered in favor of Pérez.

Reynaldo smiled widely. He looked over at Pérez sitting next to him at the counsel's table and held his hand out. Pérez's huge rough hand grabbed Reynaldo's and shook it vigorously.

"Ganamos," Reynaldo whispered loudly in his ear. Juan smiled with tears coming to his eyes.

Judge Zapata polled the jurors. This was a procedure that was the lawyers' duty, but the judge frequently took the initiative. Everyone was always trying to cover their tracks and assure that the Appellate Court would not overturn the jury verdict, and Judge Zapata was no exception.

One by one, he questioned them. "Is this your verdict?" And one by one, the jurors answered in the affirmative.

"Well, that being the case, I thank you for your work, you have been an exemplary jury, you have done a good job," Judge Zapata told the jury.

"Your honor," Reynaldo stood before the bench. "The plaintiff moves for judgment on the verdict."

"Yes, ah, yes, I think so. Judgment will be rendered for the plaintiff. Mr. García will prepare the form of the judgment. Please give Mr. Cantu a copy of the judgment so he can voice objection if he chooses. The court's adjourned until tomorrow at nine o'clock."

The judge left the courtroom, and the lawyers put their papers and books away. The jury was advised that their check for service as jurors would be mailed to them, and they casually left the courtroom.

Pérez invited Reynaldo to join him and his family for supper at the Hotel Club. Reynaldo called Mari Lou to inform her that they would be joining the Pérez family for dinner.

As Reynaldo turned to leave, he almost bumped into Mario. Each instinctively put their hands out to congratulate the other on a good job.

"Rey you did a good job, but you know that I won't let the verdict sit. I am going to appeal to the Court of Appeals, and try and get the verdict reversed," Mario said.

"Come on Mario, why waste our time and money. This record is solid, there is no error in this trial and verdict. It's going to be such a waste," Reynaldo responded with obvious displeasure, turning and walking out of the courtroom, shaking his head.

The Garcías and the Pérez family went over the entire trial about ten times, blow by blow. The whiskey and beer flowed, everyone had a good time. At midnight Reynaldo and Mari Lou begged permission to leave.

"I have a little trial tomorrow at the county court at law. I haven't even seen the file for ten days, so I better be going," Reynaldo said to Pérez.

"Well, I certainly understand. I think you attorneys are crazy. Never leave any time for rest and relaxation. You guys are crazy," Pérez said with a laugh.

If he only knew how right he was, Reynaldo thought to himself as he and his wife left the restaurant.

Chapter Twenty-nine

The week after the trial was hectic for Reynaldo. It was actually very depressing to come back to a massive mound of work. The deadlines and pressure were literally sickening. After putting out a few emergency fires, the first order of business was to prepare the form of the Pérez judgment. It consisted of listing the findings made by the jury and then stating that, based on the findings, the judge pronounced the verdict correctly. The decision by the jury was that Pérez was given possession of the disputed two hundred acres.

The form of the judgment was sent over to Mario for approval as to form and substance. Surprisingly Mario had no objections to it and returned it with his signature.

The form of the judgment was submitted to the judge for his signature, a process that usually took three minutes, but with Judge Zapata, it took three days. The judge insisted that his staff compare the form of the judgment with the jury verdict, and to other parts of the record, then give him their OK. Only then did he feel comfortable in affixing his signature to the form.

After the judgment was signed, a copy was sent immediately to the attorneys, thus giving the losing party the opportunity to begin the appellate process if necessary.

Mario and Flores had discussed the matter of the appeal at length. Mario explained the uphill battle in detail, and the remote possibility of prevailing on appeal, but Flores, a millionaire downtown merchant, could afford the attorney's fees and was not going to take the defeat lightly. He insisted on the appeal and advised Mario that it should be taken beyond the Court of Appeals to the Texas Supreme Court, if necessary.

"You have to understand Larry, that our chances on appeal are very slim. You see, mainly the only matters that I can attack are that there really was not any good, competent evidence from the witness stand to support the jury verdict, or that if there was some evidence, it was a lot more evidence against the jury verdict. If the Appellate Court agrees with me that there was no evidence from the witness stand to support the jury verdict, then they agree that the judge should not have even let the jury have the case, and Judge Zapata should have declared as a matter of law, that we were entitled to judgment. He could have done this at the end of the testimony and granted a directed verdict. He could have told them to go into the jury room and come back with a decision for us, or he could have done it at the end of the jury verdict, and granted my motion for judgment notwithstanding the verdict. That is called a judgment non obstante veredicto in Latin, or as we lawyers call it judgment NOV. So, if the appellate judges agree that there was no evidence to support the verdict they will do what the judge in the trial court should have done, and they will render judgment for you, that is called reversing and rendering the judgment. Reaching the judgment that the trial judge should have rendered.

"If the appellate judges think that there was evidence going both ways, and that the great weight and preponderance of the evidence was in our favor, but that the judge still did not grant judgment for us, then they will only reverse and remand for a new trial.

"Those are the two possibilities that we are looking at. Personally, I think that we have an excellent chance. You were in possession for eleven years. The Pérez family never questioned your possession.

Of course they claim that they did not know that you possessed their two hundred acres, but in my opinion, and from the way that I read the case law, I don't think that helps them. The main thing that hurts you is that you did, in fact, just lay behind the log, and didn't tell anyone that you were claiming the property. But I think I can overcome that with your long uninterrupted possession," Mario paused. "Well, there you have it in a nutshell. The decision to appeal is yours, you tell me what you want to do."

"No, I'm not going to let some poor shit-kicker push me around. I've got the money to fight, lots of it. And if you think we even have a small chance, I want to fight it. Go ahead and appeal. Do the best job that you know how to do. Go for it," Flores directed his attorney.

Mario went to work on the appeal almost immediately. Appellate work was unlike other legal work, primarily because it would not wait for other work. There were very stringent deadlines to meet. One slight slip up and the appeal was lost. The appellant was the party making the appeal, and the appellee was the person defending the lower court verdict.

The appellant had thirty days to give notice of appeal, and direct the district clerk to prepare all of the papers and documents that had been filed with the court in the lawsuit, called the transcript, and send them to the Appellate Court. Next, the appellant had to request the court reporter to prepare the statement of facts which included transcribing from shorthand and electronic recorder to writing all of the testimony taken from the witness stand.

Filing of the transcript and an appellate bond "perfected the appeal." This meant that the appellant had met the primary and essential deadlines, and the only things lacking was the statement of fact, known as the SOF, and the preparation of the appellate brief by both of the attorneys. Finally, of course, the attorneys filed the briefs, argued the case in front of three of the appellate justices, and waited for their decision.

The entire process took months, and sometimes a couple of years. The matter that took the longest was the preparation of the statement of facts and after that the flow of the cases through the Appellate Court. It took about six months for the court reporter to prepare the statement of facts. After that, the attorneys had sixty days to prepare the briefs, and then it took another nine months to a year for the case to be submitted to the three judges.

Reynaldo received Mario's notice of appeal, the cost bond, and direction to the district clerk to prepare the transcript. He called his client in to discuss the matter.

"Juan, they are going to appeal the case that means that we must continue to fight. Unfortunately, this means more attorney's fees," Reynaldo told his client.

Pérez winced at the mention of more expenditure. Reynaldo explained the process.

"When we go to San Antonio, I will argue to the three judges that they should leave the jury verdict and the judge's judgment on the verdict, alone. That the judgment is perfect and free of error. After we argue to the judges, then it will still take another six to eighteen months before we finally hear from them. The whole process will take from eighteen to thirty-six months," Reynaldo explained.

"Now of course, if you don't want to spend any more money, and if we do not actively pursue the appeal, they will win by default, and the judgment will be reversed. So you need to tell me whether to go ahead with the appeal or not," Reynaldo told Pérez.

"Hell yes. We've gone this far, I cannot give up now. Even if I have spent more on attorney's fees than the land is worth, I cannot give up now. That fat sonofabitch is not going to beat me by default, he's gonna have to pay just like I have," Pérez answered with rage. "Go ahead. I expect you to fight it hard all the way, even if we go to the Texas Supreme Court. I only wish it weren't so damn expensive. I'm sure I'm sending one of your children to college."

"No, Juan, if you knew how expensive it is to run a law office, you would realize that there is very little that I get to take home to my family. If it were not for my outside investments, I would be hard pressed to send my children to school, much less college. I have been lucky with some of my investments, but if it weren't for that, I just don't know," Reynaldo shook his head.

Reynaldo was not surprised when he saw the documents that he received in the mail from Mario, but he was disappointed. Reynaldo did not understand why Mario took such a ludicrous step, other than to try and play politics with the Appellate Court. Since they were teenagers, Mario had loved playing politics, and through the years had become quite a manipulator. This was the only possibility, Reynaldo thought to himself, because he knew that the evidence amply supported the verdict. Reynaldo felt like he had whipped Mario and Flores soundly.

After thinking about the appeal some more, Reynaldo asked his secretary to call Juan Pérez and tell him to come to the office to go over the matter further. Even though they had discussed it before, Reynaldo wanted to make sure that his client understood the expense that was going to be involved.

Two hours later Pérez came to the law office dressed in a khaki shirt and pants and was sweaty and smelly. He had been working cattle all day, and his work had been interrupted. Reynaldo asked him into the library. The two men sat across the table from each other as Reynaldo explained the appellate process to his client.

"If they win on appeal, we could either end up with a new trial, or the Appellate Court can render judgment against you. If we lose in the Appellate Court, then the only recourse is to apply to the Supreme Court of Texas for a review of the Appellate Court decision," Reynaldo told his client.

"Now let me explain carefully. Mario has to prove either that there was no evidence to support the jury verdict, a proposition that I feel will be impossible for him to prove, or, he must show that there was evidence going both ways and that the high weight and preponderance of the evidence favored Flores. He then must show the court that the jury disregarded the dominant evidence and granted a verdict to you instead.

"If the Appellate Court agrees with him, then they will reverse the trial court judgment. If there were no evidence, they would render judgment instead, and their action will stand in place of the trial court judgment. If they decide that there was insufficient evidence because the jury favored us in light of evidence going both ways, then the jurors should have ruled for Flores, then they will reverse and remand, which means they will direct that we have another trial here in Webb County.

"Now the important thing for you to understand is that we still have not finished. We have a lot of work ahead, and unfortunately, that means a lot of attorney's fees still ahead to be charged and paid. I know you are very sensitive about this, so I want to make sure you understand what will happen," Reynaldo said, pausing for his client to respond.

"Damn sonofabitch, why in the hell can't they admit that they tried to steal the two hundred acres from me, and give 'em back. Just because the bastard is a millionaire, he's going to fight me, punch for punch, and sweat me out," Pérez growled. "Damn sonofabitch, what a bastard. Let me think for a moment."

Pérez was visibly shaken.

The two men sat in the library. Neither spoke for several moments. Reynaldo leafed through and organized the file. After while, Pérez spoke up.

"Well, I don't have a choice. I have already gone this far. I have spent a lot of money, more money than I thought I would spend, and more money than the damn land is worth. I am not going to give in now. I swear, I should have done what that guy in Duval County did, and approached him with a forty-five and threatened to kill him if he didn't give me my land back.

"But I guess it's too late for that now, not that I would have done it anyway. So let's do it. Go for it, even if it costs more. Hell I've paid for that land twice already, so one more time won't hurt."

"All right, now let me explain briefly what is going to take place. Mario has filed a Motion for a new trial pointing out several areas where he contends that the court has erred," Reynaldo told his client, and proceeded to cover the same ground Mario had covered with Flores. "He has taken each of the individual issues, the questions that the jury answered, and contends that there either was no evidence or there was insufficient evidence to support the jury verdict," Reynaldo explained to his client, and continued with more explanations.

"Now, what will happen is that the judge will review the motion, and if he grants the action, then we start all over again here in the trial court. If he overrules Mario's challenge, then that starts the appellate process. Or else, if he does not act on the proposal for forty-five days after its filing, the action is overruled automatically, and that starts the appellate process.

"Assuming the motion is overruled then, Mario has to order the court reporter to prepare the statement of facts, which contains all the testimony in the entire trial. And then Mario has to request the transcript from the district clerk which includes all the papers that have been filed in the case. Then both of these requests are presented with the clerk of the appeals court, together with a small cash bond. Then there is a deadline set for filing the briefs.

"The briefs are nothing more than a written form of all the legal argument that a party wants to bring to the attention of the appellate judges. In summary, the areas or points that were used in the motion for new trial are usually used again, only this time they are called points of error. The attorneys argue in writing with both the facts that came out in the trial, and with the law, urging the court to agree with their argument. Of course, I will file a brief on your behalf, urging the court to leave the judgment alone, arguing to them that there was sufficient evidence, and under the law, that the trial court did not commit an error.

"We follow all these complex rules, but in essence, all that is involved is asking the Appellate Court to see if things were done correctly in the trial court. I can't for the life of me see where there is an error in this case; I cannot believe that this case will be reversed." Reynaldo concluded.

"OK. I understand. Give it all you got. Let me give you a payment on my account," Pérez said as he stood up to leave and reached in his back pocket for his checkbook. "I swear I know I'm going to send one of your children to college."

Aside for the time that it took, Reynaldo loved appellate work. There was little thinking on your feet, no immediate pressure, no immediate stress, no adrenaline flowing. You sat in your library with all the midnight oil in the world, and you read all the cases on point that you could find. It was a question of reading and logically defending the jury verdict.

The procedure was that the appellant filed his brief first, since he had the burden of proof. Then the appellee replied, and the appellant had the opportunity to submit a counter-reply brief. Mario went through all the hoops, and Reynaldo responded to each one. Mario complained that the trial court had erred, because there was no evidence or because there was insufficient to support all the elements of the jury verdict. Therefore the trial court erred in its judgment. The format of the appellant's brief was a listing of the points of error and then under each point of error he supported his position with an argument in writing, bolstered with case law on each of his points. The appellee's brief was similar with a listing of reply points, backed-up with his own legal precedents.

Reynaldo enjoyed the preparation of the brief tremendously. He was, after all, a frustrated writer, having longed for years to write a book, or a novel, or a book of short stories. To Reynaldo, the brief was a work of art that he was always extremely proud of and showed off to his secretary, family, and colleagues.

The process took months. Eventually, the court reporter was ready with the statement of facts. It consisted of five thick volumes, of question and answer testimony, and court comments, and attorney statements, objections and arguments.

After the statement of facts was prepared, the attorneys spent hours reading the transcript over, and over, and over, again. After the research, it was time for writing and rewriting, and rewriting. After about ten drafts, the brief was finally ready for filing. Once the brief was filed, it took months for the court to acknowledge that the case was ripe for submission.

The first notification was to advise the attorneys which three judges were assigned to hear the case. Then, months later the attorneys were informed of when they would be given the opportunity to submit oral arguments. After filing their briefs, the attorneys usually forgot about the case until a couple of weeks before submission, when preparation for oral argument began in earnest.

Chapter Thirty

Months went by and Reynaldo slaved away at his legal duties. He had practiced law for sixteen years now, and he often wondered if he had picked the wrong profession. The stress was intolerable. The return on investment was awful. Clients typically did not pay well. He could be hard-nosed and demand thousands of dollars in advance, of course, but he rarely was able to be so callused.

He did not need the money since his partnership in the RiverView housing development had done exceptionally well. He and Bernie Velez were both millionaires as a result of RiverView, but Reynaldo had not dreamed and worked selfishly for years to become a real estate developer; he had starved and slaved to become a lawyer. He had enjoyed the paper chase, he had loved it.

Law school prepared him well to do his work, but it had not explained the business challenges. At times he hated his job. He felt guilty for disliking it, and that made it worse. He hated getting calls at home, and often almost cursed clients for calling him there. It spilled over to the office, and at times he even disliked to get clients calling him at the office. He often remembered his old friend George Abromowitz at the former law firm who frequently said that "The practice of law would be just fine if it weren't for the clients; if it weren't for the dumb clients who keep bothering you. If I didn't have to keep talking to the clients, I could handle the case just fine."

Reynaldo knew that his children idolized him, and the feeling was mutual. They often spoke of becoming lawyers just like their father. He did not want them to follow him. Then again, the profession had been kind to him, it had helped him out of poverty, and had established him prominently in his community. The days seemed to come more and more frequently now when he felt like walking out of the office and not coming back for months.

The only thing that kept him going were the deadlines, which were plentiful, and which he could not stop or postpone. If he did not have a deadline, a court setting, or some work to complete, he usually felt miserable.

Perhaps, if the children did want to become lawyers, it would not be wrong. Or if they specialized, and lived in a big city, where there would be plenty of clients, plenty of money, and camaraderie. Perhaps, he thought.

At times he sat in the library and reminisced about the past sixteen years. The first five were training, the second five involved working from dawn till dusk, and the third five years were supposed to be settling down to the lifetime career, but culminated in frustration.

He didn't have to practice law anymore but felt he just could not leave the law, it would be like abandoning a good and faithful wife. It could not be done. If he did, it would be a sin, he confessed to himself many times. The treasonous act would lead to bad luck for sure, he thought. Maybe after practicing twenty years he would decide, but not now. In a few more years, maybe.

Strangely he knew that his colleagues were going through the same kind of hell. On one occasion he dropped his guard, and complained a little, ever so slightly, but then shut up and slaved through another hard, stressful, fateful day. He knew that he did not want to die unhappy and that someday he would quit, whether it seemed ungrateful or not, whether it brought bad luck or not. It just was not worth it, and life already seemed too short.

Because of the strain, stress, and frustration, he sometimes compared his career to life and felt that he had already run a good race, and it was time for it to come to a natural end. Who could criticize? Who could complain? He was an excellent lawyer, an excellent businessman. He had lived three lives in one already. If his career ended who would notice, who could criticize him, who would or could feel sorry and have pity? Certainly not Mari Lou, she would love for him to retire and spend more time with her and the children. But somehow, as good as that sounded, he could not bring himself to take the steps needed to escape.

He caught himself thinking of the negative side of his profession and got back to work. The days, weeks, and months continued to go by. It seemed that time went too fast, but deep inside he felt it was not fast enough. He yearned for the time when it would all be over and he could enjoy life.

He started noticing this phenomenon one cold January before he realized it was March and the annual celebration of the Fiesta de San Jose was upon him. Before he knew it, Easter, came and then suddenly it was the end of the school year. This was quickly followed by an insufferable hot summer, Thanksgiving, Christmas, New Year, and another year went by. The years went by too fast. They looked and felt just like the other. Each year seemed as joyless as the other.

One day he got a card from the Court of Appeals in San Antonio notifying him that the three-judge panel would hear arguments in the *Flores v. Pérez* case. The panel was composed of Justices Pasquel, Sánchez, and Larvin. Those three judges would decide whether the jury verdict had been in error or not.

Reynaldo did not give it much thought. He felt he had a good case, and it really did not matter who the three judges were. All he wanted was three learned and fair judges. Nevertheless, the notice caused him to bring out the file and review every part of it, from beginning to end. He spent the whole day going over all parts of it. He took notes and started to prepare the oral argument he needed to make before the judges. It had been about a year now since the jury verdict, which was not uncommon. It took another three months before oral arguments, and another six months after that before the Appellate Court handed down its final decision.

Right on schedule, three months later he got a notice to appear before the Appellate Court in San Antonio and present his oral argument. Reynaldo always left for San Antonio the day before the hearing, because he wanted to be rested when he made his argument to the court. Usually, the court heard three cases in the morning and three in the afternoon. He had never drawn an afternoon argument. He had appeared in several hearings in the Court of Appeals and had not lost an appeal yet.

Although the daily grind of his work was frustrating, Reynaldo liked appellate work, because it mostly involved him and his law books, with very little involvement by clients or opposing counsel. He sat down at his favorite library table and read, read, and read some more until finally, everything gelled and resulted in a masterpiece brief. He loved it.

The briefs were filed with the court, and supposedly by the time oral arguments came, the three justices had read them and understood the case. The attorneys lived with the briefs for at least three days before making their final argument and knew theirs and their opponent's position thoroughly.

Chapter Thirty-one

eynaldo and Mari Lou drove to San Antonio where they planned to meet Juan Pérez and his wife. True to form, the old cowboy was waiting for him in the hotel lobby. The two couples ate dinner together that night. Reynaldo went over what would happen in court the following day so they knew what to expect.

"First, Mario will get up and argue his position. He gets to go first because he is the appellant, and he has the burden of proving the trial court and the jury wrong. He argues for twenty minutes or so, and then I get up and argue for about thirty minutes. Mario then gets ten minutes to refute what I have said. Again, he gets the advantage to close, because he has the burden of proving the trial court was wrong. It's really rather fast. Before you realize it, it is all over," Reynaldo explained and continued to tell his clients about the process.

"Maybe we won't be the first case, then you can see other lawyers go through the motions, and when you see ours, it will be clearer. Sometimes you come with all your argument planned out, and then the judges take over and start asking you questions, one right after another, and you are never able to get back to your planned presentation, and your argument," Reynaldo told his clients.

"Again, one thing you have to realize Juan is that it is impossible to predict what those three brains are thinking, and what they will finally decide. We think that we have this thing whipped, and it's pretty close to over, but we just don't know. We just don't know," Reynaldo explained.

"In the morning we'll meet for breakfast and walk across the street, go up to the third floor and get after it. Now eat well, because tomorrow we may be too nervous," Reynaldo laughed.

Reynaldo stayed up late going over the briefs and his argument but was awake by five o'clock. He awoke Mari Lou at six, and by seven they were having breakfast with his clients. They had to be in court by eight-thirty. They chatted over breakfast, and Reynaldo gave them a short preview of his argument. Pérez loved it. He was mesmerized. All his life he had envied educated men, those with the schooling that he never got. He did not realize the importance of education until he was older when it was too late for him. After this realization, he loved it when someone's education really shone through and touched him. He vowed to make sure his children got a university or college education.

After breakfast, the group strolled across the street to the five-story baroque, red stone building that had served as the courthouse for some one hundred years. It was a large and magnificent structure. The group went up in the elevator and exited on the third floor where Reynaldo signed in with the clerk of the court, and they all walked into the beautifully appointed courtroom. It was surrounded with portraits of all the justices that had served on the court. There was wood everywhere. Heavy wooden benches resembling church pews, a large elevated desk for the three judges, and lush, thick carpet on the floor. The room was brightly lit.

Reynaldo got his material out of the briefcase and waited. He had determined that he was number two, which meant that one case would be argued before theirs. He was glad of this because Mari Lou and his clients would get an extra treat.

Minutes later Mario and Larry showed up. Reynaldo, Mari Lou, and the Pérezes exchanged greetings with Mario. Flores refused to greet them. He moved over to one side of the courtroom and pouted, as he waited for the session to open.

Once their case was called, the action moved fast. Mario nicked away at the alleged error committed by the jury and by Judge Zapata. Reynaldo was not impressed. Reynaldo surveyed the court and caught Judges Sánchez's and Pasquel's eyes. It seemed ever so slightly that they wanted to wink to greet him.

Reynaldo followed with a very impressive argument, rebutting Mario on every point. He stared at the Judges' eyes, and none turned their eyes away. He felt that was a good sign. Mario closed with nothing new, just adding a couple of cute remarks to which, under the rules, Reynaldo could not respond.

The García and Pérez families had lunch together and made separate preparations to drive back to Laredo.

"Juan, again, I cannot predict what will happen, but frankly I can't see what Mario did to hurt us. I feel just great about the argument. I am going to be extremely disappointed if the Court elects to overturn the judgment. Let's just pray and wait. It will be about a year before we hear from the court."

"Reynaldo I agree with you about what the court should do. I don't understand things the way you do, but I did not feel like he hurt us a bit. I think you argued very well Reynaldo. I felt great about the way you explained things. We'll just have to see," Pérez said, obviously pleased.

When Reynaldo opened the office the next morning he checked his phone messages. He was surprised to find one cryptic message from San Antonio, which had been received in the office about four in the afternoon. It read, "Judge Pete Sánchez called from the Appellate Court in San Antonio, he says not to worry. Do not respond."

He knew of course that it was Pete Sánchez and he wondered why the judge had to play that way. Reynaldo knew that if he complained to the judge for doing it, that the judge would call him naive and stupid. There was no way to change him, Reynaldo thought. It was several months before he heard on the case again.

Usually, after an appellate argument, Reynaldo took on a high and gradually descend in about twenty-four hours. Then, he felt burned out and unable to energetically attack his deadlines. It took until the following Monday to get going strong again.

At the Court of Appeals, the Chief Justice assigned a case to one justice on a three-judge panel, who in turn assigned the case to a briefing attorney, also called a law clerk. The justice informed the clerk about how he generally felt the case should turn, and it was the clerk's job to research and either agree or disagree with the justice. After the justice had a typewritten opinion, the clerk sent it to the other justices, and requested that they either concur or dissent. If one of the justices was to dissent, he submitted a dissenting opinion.

In *Flores v. Pérez*, the chief judge assigned the opinion to Justice Arnold Larvin. It was his duty to produce the first opinion which the other judges either accepted as the majority opinion or became the dissenting opinion if the other two justices disagreed with it.

Judge Sánchez was determined to help Reynaldo and took it upon himself to write an opinion, hoping that he could convince the rest of the panel to follow his lead.

"I tell you, I don't see how the appellant can win this case," Judge Sánchez told his briefing attorney. "I have scrutinized the record, and there is simply no reason why this case should go to the appellant. Now, I suspect that Justice Larvin will go for the appellant, so I want you to hurry with a good dissenting opinion, and maybe we can talk to him and Judge Pasquel to come along. Get busy."

* * * *

The months went by, and things went along as usual at Reynaldo's office. On occasion, he thought of the appellate argument and the fact he was still waiting on the decision. He thought of appealing to the Supreme Court if he did not win at the Fourth Court in San Antonio. He thought of Pérez, who would complain about the cost and expense of going any farther with the case.

Eight months after the appellate argument he kept an eye open for Thursday mail. The Appellate court published and mailed its decisions on Wednesday, which reached Laredo by Thursday afternoon.

Reynaldo usually went home for lunch. It was a nice advantage that small towns had over large cities. A person could go home for lunch, and take a short nap and still be back at the office by one fifteen. Things were slow, small, uncomplicated, and traffic was always light.

On occasion, Mari Lou went shopping or to a meeting of one kind or another, or to go see her sister or mother in San Diego. When this happened, Reynaldo had lunch at the Plaza Hotel, the best buffet in town. The price couldn't be beaten anywhere, and the food, though not gourmet, was wholesome. On the day he was waiting for the decision from the Court of Appeals he went to lunch at the Plaza and afterward walked to the post office to see if the decision was in the mail and also to see which clients sent checks.

He walked in the clear bright and hot day. He took advantage of the shade trees as he walked to the massive granite building. He slipped the key into his mailbox lock, opened it and pulled out all the envelopes with mail. He found two checks, and then he saw it. The envelope bore the seal of the Fourth Court of Appeals. It was the Pérez decision, and he felt happy, he knew it would be positive.

He could not wait to get back to the office to open it, so he walked over to a customer work table in the post office lobby and clenching his teeth tore the envelope open. He quickly read the short transmittal letter and then began to read the entire opinion thoroughly.

The first two pages went over the facts and reviewed the lower court decision, and the appellant's argument and position, then the opinion took an awkward turn. The opinion was written by Justice Larvin, and he favored Mario. Reynaldo read hurriedly through the opinion. Judge Larvin determined that there was no evidence to support the jury findings. "Not insufficient evidence, or an imbalance of evidence, not a finding of prejudice or passion by the jury in voting for Pérez, but no evidence!" Reynaldo angrily thought as he continued reading in disbelief. He saw that Judge Pasquel joined or concurred with Judge Larvin. At the end of the opinion was a lengthy dissenting opinion by Judge Sánchez. The dissenting opinion was good, and precisely what Reynaldo hoped the majority opinion should have been.

What in the world happened? He was shocked. He had to go call his client. But first, he went to the office and reread the opinion slowly. Maybe he missed something. But how could it be, he read the conclusion. Reynaldo hated to lose. Anytime he lost, even a minor pre-trial motion it took hours for him to feel good again.

Reynaldo informed his secretary that the Court of Appeals had gone against him in the Pérez case. She knew it was going to be a long, depressing afternoon.

Reynaldo read the opinion again, slowly. He still could not understand why the justices had gone against him. The court was saying that there was absolutely no evidence to support the jury verdict. No evidence to support the finding that Flores had not claimed the property, no evidence to support the conclusion that his possession of the property had not been continuous, adverse nor hostile. The court was saying there was no evidence to support the finding that he did not make improvements on the land. "Hell," Reynaldo fumed, "each of the issues, or questions, was amply supported by testimony from Larry Flores himself." He shook his head in disbelief.

He wondered what he should do? Should he call Judge Sánchez? No, it was unethical, he would not do that. It was a something he had never done, and he was not going to start now.

Reynaldo asked the secretary to call Juan Pérez. He had to break the news to the client. Pérez was not in, and Reynaldo left word for him to come to the office the following morning.

By the next morning, Reynaldo had calmed down from the defeat, although he still could not understand the why of the court decision. He read it again and again, in disbelief.

Pérez came in at ten o'clock, and the two men sat in the library sipping coffee. Reynaldo explained the decision in detail.

"Believe me, Juan, this is wrong. I don't know why, or how they could come up with this decision. All I can tell you is, it's wrong," Reynaldo told his client. "You can take the whole record to ten attorneys, and I guarantee you that the ten would tell you that this decision is wrong, wrong, wrong! There's very little I can do now except ask for a rehearing which is seldom granted, and then appeal to the Supreme Court. You tell me what you want to do. Unfortunately, it will cost the attorney's fees to keep fighting. You tell me what to do, it's your decision."

There was a long silence, as Pérez read the opinion. After ten minutes, he spoke up.

"Nah, nah. I hate to admit it, but I'm whipped. I spent so much on this land already, more than its market value. I'm not going any farther. That's it. They whipped us! Someday, somehow, things will even up. Like the Anglos say 'what goes around comes around,' and Larry Flores will pay for his misdeed, either here or upstairs, but that's it. I won't appeal to the Texas Supreme Court. It's over," Pérez said in apparent dejection.

There was quiet again. Reynaldo held his head low in defeat. Juan just kept reading the opinion.

"Reynaldo, please make me a copy of this, I want to take it home and cry on it," Pérez said with a smile and a wink.

"Incidentally Reynaldo, I don't want you to feel bad. I want you to know that I feel you did the best damn job possible. I have absolutely no regrets as far as your work is concerned. I am proud of what you did and how you did it. So don't hold your head down. You did just great," Pérez told Reynaldo. "It's just that some big old monster that we don't know how to deal with got us and he hurt us bad. But seriously Rey, I don't regret a damn thing. You did great. About the only thing I regret is having to contribute to educating one or two of your kids. You be sure they go to a good school, you hear."

Pérez stood, smiled, dusted off his hat, and shook hands with Reynaldo.

Chapter Thirty-two

Nothing helped snap Reynaldo out of a bad feeling and mood better than hard work and the ever-present deadlines that he could not ignore. Such was the case for May and June. He was so busy, he hardly had time to raise his head, and look around. He had very little time to think about the Pérez defeat, and the appellate decision, disregarding two years of excellent research and trial work. He told himself that someday he would learn what happened, and why. In the meantime, he could not afford to spend time worrying about a situation that was out of his hands.

He worked and worked some more on trials that seemed to go unending. He worked on another appeal. This more than anything reminded him of the Pérez case. In a short time, he forced himself to forget the Pérez case, or else he would neglect the work at hand.

As summer approached, Reynaldo looked forward to the warm weather and a vacation with Mari Lou and the children. But primarily to the fact that things slowed down a little at the courthouse, and other offices. Courts staff and judges took vacations, and this slowed the pace and it was enjoyable for a change.

In July, of course, they looked forward to the RiverView July 4th Annual Party. He recalled when Bernie Velez had first proposed for them to sponsor this shindig.

Velez had always enjoyed rubbing elbows with the bigwigs. He loved to socialize and be around the politicians and the movers and shakers. His experiences at the plaza shining shoes and hearing the men plan political and commercial strategy had given him a yearning that he vowed to duplicate.

The success of RiverView Hills made it possible for Velez's dreams to come true. He always managed to keep his finger in politics, and to contribute in time and money to the political system. He was a barrio person, and kept close tabs on what was going on, where, and why, and by whom. Because of his involvement and his sincere concern for fairness and progress, and his prominent position in the barrios, he was always sought out by the powerful politicians or their representatives. They valued his input on what was good for the barrios, and what was good for them.

When he skyrocketed to riches and affluence, all politicians knew it was only a matter of time before he took a very active role in making things happen. They were not wrong, as he began actively participating in local, regional, and state politics immediately. It became his favorite hobby. He attended to business fervently and tenaciously, but it seemed that daily he got tremendous pleasure, satisfaction, and relaxation from being able to pick up the phone and talk to the governor, of Texas or a Mexican state. Also to his senator and representative, state or national. Others, similarly situated, completed the circle of his new-found fraternity brothers. He loved every minute of it.

One day Velez called Reynaldo and asked him to drop by his office, which was located on the fringe of the RiverView development and anchored the recreational park complex that Velez had built. The park was beautifully landscaped. It had three baseball parks, two swimming pools, four tennis courts, four racquetball courts, a massive pavilion for dances and outdoor presentations.

Velez felt that RiverView had been so good to him he had to return the favor, and the park was his way to show his appreciation. One day he asked Reynaldo for his opinion on an idea he had to show his gratitude.

"Reynaldo my good friend. I want to discuss something with you and see what you think," Velez said to Reynaldo as they took their seats in the office. "You are my partner, so I want to ask you something. I want to have a huge July 4th party. It will probably cost about $50,000, but I want bands playing music, throughout the party; I want to serve steaks, food and drink that people want. I want to serve fancy food, and I want fireworks and watermelon, and get this, get this, I want to invite all of the important people in this county, surrounding counties, the state of Texas, and even Washington and Mexico. What do you think?"

"I guess it would be nice. Wow, super fancy. Why do you ask me?" Reynaldo inquired.

"The reason I ask you is that RiverView will give the party, and that means you and me, which means that half of the money will come out of your pocket. You have to say yes, or else I have to give the party by myself, and not under the name of RiverView Hills. That's all, twenty-five grand comes out of your pocket," Velez explained.

"Well, I've never been actively involved in politics the way you have Bernie, but if you want this party, and if you feel it's important, then I have never been one to worry much about money anyway. If I did I would have quit practicing law a long, long time ago. Go for it. Just one special favor. Don't make it in my name. I can't divorce myself from RiverView Hills, that's you and me, and I'm part of it, just don't make it in the name of Bernie and Rey, nor Bernardo Velez and Reynaldo García. I like to keep a low profile if I can. What do you think?" Reynaldo asked his partner.

"Absolutely no problem. That's just fine. Damn you're a good partner. I have never had any problem with you whatever. I am a lucky man indeed. Can you just think of all the partnerships that have had so many, many problems? Damn, we're lucky we get along so well," Velez said smiling from ear to ear.

From the very beginning, it was understood, that all partnership property was to be owned fifty-fifty and that Velez would take care of operations, and Reynaldo would take care of things in the background, the details, the law, the problems. This was the way they agreed to it, and this was the way it was set up and the way that each wanted it.

So it was, and Velez went forward with the first Fourth of July Party. A huge extravaganza that was hard to forget for the rest of the year.

The party became a Laredo tradition and was always the highlight of the summer. As short as the party was, it was enjoyable, especially meeting new people from other parts of the state and the country. Even Reynaldo, as much of an introvert that he was, enjoyed the 4th of July Party.

This year the weather was not as hot as usual. The thermometer stood at an even eighty degrees, and in Laredo, Texas that was cool. Maybe not cool, but it was definitely not hot. It might not be very comfortable for the Washington people, but to the Austinites, it would be tolerable, and for Laredoans, it was delightful.

Reynaldo and Mari Lou walked on the lush green grass and looked for friends under the tall shade trees. Friends were not hard to find. Soon they settled with a crowd, and talked, and drank beer. The music played, and children screamed. Firecrackers popped. There was a smell of gunpowder, and barbecue in the air. After a while, Reynaldo excused himself to go find Bernie Velez and saw him with a group of Washington D. C. staffers. They were enjoying one another, the group of Yankees entirely charmed by the self-made Mexican millionaire. They were talking about going to Mexico and buying knick-knacks, rum, tequila, and other curios. The visitors were amazed at how easy it was to cross over into a completely foreign country. Velez introduced Reynaldo, and the two men and the small group exchanged conversation for about thirty minutes.

By the time Reynaldo got back to Mari Lou, it was time to eat, and the group walked to the food line. They walked slowly through the buffet and loaded up on meat, beans, and rice. It was not a good Mexican fiesta without the beans, Reynaldo thought. This year Velez insisted on preparing something special, and that was corn gorditas, fat little corn tortillas cooked on a grill, then deep fried, split open and stuffed with guisado, refried beans, or guacamole. When people found out gorditas were being served, they immediately came back for seconds and soon there was a bottleneck. The visitors could not get enough.

The Garcías and their group sat under one of the enormous oak trees, and ate lunch quietly, listening to the music. After lunch, the men got watermelon and ice cream for the ladies. The group sat lazily around under the tree and took life easy.

After a couple of hours, Reynaldo helped Velez play host to the out of town visitors. He told Mari Lou where he was going and vowed to return in two hours, at which time they would decide whether to leave or stay for more of the festivities.

Reynaldo walked casually around the grounds, greeting friends and strangers alike. He had already consumed a few beers, and felt happy and a little loose. After finally finding Velez they talked and politicked with several Austin officials. All were having a grand time, and most congratulated Velez on the party and hoped he continued the tradition. The RiverView July 4th Party in Laredo had achieved statewide and national recognition and at least those present pleaded with Velez to keep having the party.

Reynaldo split off. It was about four thirty in the afternoon. Shadows were beginning to get longer, there was more shade now. The crowd had slowly swelled to approximately a thousand, making their way slowly around the park, through the loud murmur, screaming Tejano and country and western music, and the smell of the smoke, food, and meat cooking.

As Reynaldo walked by one of the open bars, he noticed Judge Pete Sánchez. He had not seen him since the Pérez appellate argument and had not thought of him. Judge Sánchez was delighted to see Reynaldo, and Reynaldo in his usual naive way was actually happy to see the big fat man, since the hangover of the Pérez decision had finally gone away.

"Reynaldo how good to see you. Come here let me shake your hand," Judge Sánchez yelled through the small group of people that surrounded the bar area.

The two men smiled at each other, hugged and slapped each other on the back, in the Mexican abrazo custom.

"Pete it's good to see you, I hope you have been doing all right," Reynaldo said.

"Rey we've been doing great up in San Antone. My wife and kids love it, and we're just thrilled. Listen, thanks for having us. This party is just great, and everyone is talking about how much fun it is. We sure do hope that you guys keep having this party. How is your family?"

"Oh Pete, we are doing just fine. And I am glad that you are doing likewise. I'm kind of surprised to see you, I thought I would have seen you earlier. I thought you weren't here."

"We came in a little late. You know every time we get close to Laredo we have to go across the river to the Jardin Restaurant. Everyone likes the bolillos, the guacamole, and the way they cook everything. The food there is just great, and the gin fizzes are super, everyone loves 'em. So anyway that's where we were, and that's why we're late."

"That explains it. Laredoans usually stay away from Mexico, going only once or twice per year to stock up on candy and tequila," Reynaldo said to his friend, laughing heartily.

"Reynaldo, please step over here with me, I need to talk with you," Judge Sánchez grabbed Reynaldo by the elbow and took him off to the side.

"Listen, guy, I've wanted to call you and talk to you, but I just haven't been able. I want to talk to you about the Pérez decision. You saw my dissent I'm sure, and it was great, and in your favor,

I'm sure you'll agree. But I just couldn't get Roy to join me and turn the decision around, he insisted on sticking with Mario Cantu. I'm really sorry, I couldn't pull it off for you, but Roy just wouldn't help me, he wouldn't come along. Ordinarily, Roy would, but for his reasons, that wasn't the case with this one. Come on over let's find him, he has a reason, and I want him to tell you, so you don't think I'm telling you stories. Come on he's just over here."

Reynaldo kept silent, as the men walked about ten yards to where the tall, dark white-headed Judge Pasquel stood with a couple of men.

"Roy, Roy come here please," Judge Sánchez motioned to his friend and fellow judge.

Judge Pasquel politely left the other men and joined Judge Sánchez and Reynaldo.

"Roy, come over here, somebody wants to beat the crap outta you. You remember Reynaldo García from the *Flores v. Pérez* decision. Well this is the guy you fucked," Judge Sánchez laughed, as he threatened the judge playfully. "I tried to talk Roy into coming along with me on my dissent, in which case we would have been the majority, but old Roy here just wouldn't. Why don't you tell him, Roy, tell him what happened."

"Let me tell you, Reynaldo, I just had a big problem with your case. You see I wanted to be Texas Supreme Court justice so bad I could taste it when Judge Troy Turbin died. When the Democratic Committee voted in Brownsville for a successor, I was just sure that somehow I'd get the appointment. Then when the date came up, the only guy that voted for me was Mario Cantu. Can you imagine that? Outta the two hundred committeemen in the whole state of Texas, only one guy voted for a Mexican, that's Mario Cantu. So when your case came up on appeal, I agreed with Pete here. I think he properly analyzed the law and the facts, and he hit it on the money, he has it right. And if you go to the Supreme Court,

I'm sure you will win. But you see, when Mario Cantu came on up to the Court of Appeals, I had to pay back the guy a favor. Although I favored you and Pete on the law and the facts, I had to vote for Mario Cantu, because I owed him. Do you understand Reynaldo?"

Reynaldo could not believe what he was hearing. It was warm, it was getting late, and he had slugged a few beers, and he really wasn't sure that he really heard what Judge Pasquel said.

"Wow! Wait a minute. I want to make sure I understand what you said to me. I think I heard correctly, and I think I understood correctly, but will you please repeat what you just said?" Reynaldo asked incredulously.

"Oh hell, don't be a naive kid. Aren't you ever going to understand how things work, and how they work for us now, because now we're in power? I said simply, that I voted against you in the Pérez case, because I had to go with Mario Cantu, I didn't disagree with your case, and I would've voted for you if it hadn't been Mario Cantu on the other side. Do you understand? I just had to pay back a favor, he is the only guy in the entire state of Texas that had the guts to vote for me for an appointment to the Texas Supreme Court."

"Oh okay, I understand," Reynaldo was in a daze. He stayed with the small group that gathered after Judge Pasquel's confession. He pretended to be there, but he wasn't. His mind raced a million miles away. He thought of the disclosure, and the case, and his terrible disappointment in the judicial system. Finally, after a few minutes, he begged off and left.

He strolled, wanting to see Mari Lou; with an urge to cry, to scream. He thought of burning his law license. He wanted to turn back the clock and throw all the trash away. He was upset and unhappy. He shook his head as he walked through the park. Finally, he found Mari Lou.

"Reynaldo, what's wrong, honey? You look like you're going to faint. Are you all right?" Mari Lou asked.

"Yes Malu, I am doing all right. I'm okay but can we leave, and can we leave quickly?"

"Yes honey, let's go. Do you want some cold water? You look like you're getting dehydrated. You look like you might be having a heart attack."

"No honey, let's just go," he barked at her.

The couple walked through the park. She held him by the waist, and he did the same. Occasionally he noticed her looking over to see him. He could sense that she thought he was sick.

"Reynaldo, are you having a heart attack?"

Reynaldo shook his head but did not respond otherwise. As they approached the gate, Reynaldo's color looked a little better.

"Rey honey, please say something to me," Mari Lou pleaded. "Is everything all right?"

"Sonofabitch! Sonofabitch!"

"Reynaldo! Reynaldo, why are you cursing?" Mari Lou asked, shocked at her husband's demeanor.

"I'm sorry babe. I'm just so disappointed. I need to go talk to Juan Pérez and explain the great Texas legal system. Let's go."

Reynaldo tousled her hair and put his hand around her waist, and they hurried off to the parking lot.

THE END

Afterword

"Hello?"

"Hi, Dad, how are you?"

"I'm fine, mijita, how are you?"

"Good. I went to a diversity workshop today, and my homework is to do this exercise with someone I know. Will you do it with me?"

"Sure."

"Ok. I'm going to read you a series of statements, and you should answer 'yes' or 'no' after each one if it applies to you or not."

As I read the statements aloud to my father over the phone, he responded without hesitation to each.

"I can be in the company of people of my race most of the time."

"Yes."

"When I go to a job interview, one or more people of my racial background will most likely be on the hiring committee."

"Yes."

"I can be pretty sure that my neighbors will be neutral or pleasant to me."

"Yes."

"I can turn on the television or open the front page of the paper and see people of my race widely and positively represented."

"Yes."

At this, unexpectedly, I began crying.

"What's wrong mijita?"

"It's just that when I did this…I answered 'no' on most of the questions. I guess it's just been very different for me living in

Austin compared to how it is for you living in Laredo. I always feel like I have to be careful at work because I don't know if I'm being judged or not getting a promotion because of being Latina. There are no other Latinas on my team or in management."

The exercise was called "Color Lines."

During the workshop I had attended earlier that day, all the participants totaled up their scores. Everyone stood and arranged themselves into a line from the person with the lowest score to the person with the highest score. The result was undeniable. Those with the lowest scores had the darkest skin complexion, and those with the highest scores had the lightest. Social researchers have tested the exercise with consistent results.

After completing the 25-question exercise with my Dad, I thought about the results through a new lens. Dad was dark-skinned and obviously Latino, except for being exceptionally tall at six-foot-four. The population of Laredo is more than ninety-five percent Hispanic. In that environment, Dad was part of the majority racial group. His culture was represented nearly everywhere, and he didn't have to worry so much about whether he would be treated or perceived unfairly because of his race.

This perception was not prevalent in Austin, where I had gone to high school and later returned to continue my career after graduate school. Austin, in 2016, was around thirty-five percent Hispanic, and the environment in the city was geographically and socially segregated by race at the intersection of poverty.

The first time I ever read the statements in the "Color Lines" exercise, they was were framed as statements about "white privilege." Experiencing this moment with my Dad made me think that the statements tested for social representation rather than skin color. That could be true to an extent, but even Dad, who remarked that he had "thick skin" and that these things "just don't get to him," had to answer "no" to some of the statements.

"If a police officer pulls me over, I can be sure he isn't singling me out because of my race."

"I can choose blemish cover or bandages in flesh color and have them more or less match my skin."

These two statements point to the workings of our society and government. We have a hard time divorcing ourselves from society and government even if we isolate ourselves in a city where "minorities" are in the racial majority. *Judgment Reversed* explores this observation through the unavoidable context of the judicial system.

* * * *

Ricardo D. Palacios is my father. He passed away on December 15, 2018, while *Judgment Reversed* was under review by his publisher, Alfredo E. Cárdenas of MCM Books. *Judgment Reversed* is Dad's fourth published book and his second fictional work. The original manuscript was written in the '90s when I was a child. Dad had sent *Judgment Reversed* and his other novel, *Chon*, off to publishers, but they rejected the manuscripts.

Dad and I met Alfredo Cárdenas of MCM Books at an annual conference of the Tejano Genealogical Society in Austin. Dad saw in MCM Books an opportunity to realize his dream of publishing his two fictional books. At the same conference, Dad and I attended a workshop about how the Spanish colonized south Texas (before it was Texas). It was there that I learned how the Spanish had instituted a system of privilege based on race. The system was designed to encourage families in central Mexico to travel north to colonize lands in what is now Texas. Spain promised land, money, livestock, and legal privileges to families willing to undertake the arduous journey northward. The King's representatives in New Spain offered individuals or families with more Spanish heritage additional resources and rights. The stage Spanish conquistadors set for these families, who lived under the sistema de castas, is still playing out today.

RICARDO D. PALACIOS

Judgment Reversed is as relevant today as it would have been in the '90s. Despite the ending of Jim Crow laws with the passage of the Civil Rights Act in the 1960s, in 2020, we Tejanos find ourselves in a vulnerable yet powerful place as an ethnic group. Our identity is always in question. The white political establishment fears us and, at the same time, antagonizes us. We find ourselves holding various positions toward the white power structure: subjugated, defensive, or attempting to blend in with it.

To be Tejano is to be everything at once: Spanish, indigenous, German, Polish, French, Jewish, Irish, and the list goes on. The Tejano identity retains innocence and guilt as both the colonized and the colonizers. Laredoans are the epitome of the complex Tejano identity. As colonized people who crave the privilege of colonizers, we participate in a complex judicial system stacked against us. Feeling that we have no choice, we accept the violence of the legal system believing it to be somehow more peaceful than insurrection. We participate in democracy as if the rules were established in plain sight for all to see.

The League of United Latin American Citizens (LULAC), a Latino civil rights organization, has roots in Laredo and other south Texas towns and cities. While LULAC still exists to provide power and training to Latinos in the U.S., instances in its history have been paradoxically racist. In the 1930s, LULAC sought to achieve white privilege for its members by lobbying for categorization within the "white" race on the U.S. Census. The goal of this policy was not to be perceived as "black" at a time when black Americans arguably had even more hardships and fewer privileges than today.

Ta Nehisi Coates, a prominent Black author who writes about racism in the United States, refers to white people as "people who believe they are white." Coates uses this phrasing to present the concept of race as a social construct. Race is a system that defines privileges based on categories, and it exists because our culture, systems, and institutions reinforce it. It takes more than the U.S. Census to make Latinos "white" or to help us believe that we are "white."

Judgment Reversed raises real questions as to what it means to be "white." Is being "white" having the privilege of participating in the judicial system, owning land, affording higher education, running for public office? When Tejanos or Latinos achieve these things, are we tearing down systems of inequality, or are we merely submitting to a system that will always be unfair? Protagonist Reynaldo García's loss in *Judgment Reversed* is a disturbing reminder of how high the power structure stacks the cards against Latinos and all people of color in the United States. Hard work and playing by the rules pay off for us, but only up to a point.

Latinos are underrepresented in professional careers, including the judiciary, and are severely underpaid, with Latinas earning only fifty-three cents for every dollar a white male makes. Census experts project that Latinos will make up more than forty percent of the U.S. population by the year 2050. The 2020 census will tell us how close we get. This count is of great importance to the Latino population because it will help determine representation in the halls of Congress and state legislatures and will be used in the allocation of funding for Federal assistance programs.

In some ways, I believe Dad wrote this book as a way to break racist stereotypes about Mexican-Americans. Society tells us we are not intelligent, that we are lazy, or that we have no political prowess. Reynaldo's world in *Judgment Reversed* is a reflection of the life and times my father experienced. Their world provided opportunities that many other Latinos in the U.S. did not have. They were born into landowning families, a significant advantage in a society that prioritizes capital. Their education and hard work led to prosperity and stability. When I read this book, I felt that Dad wanted the dominant culture and Latinos themselves to acknowledge that they are valuable and worthy of attention; to stop marginalizing Latinos and other "minority" groups.

For Latinos, breaking stereotypes and being centered is about more than "colorblindness." We need to see our communities as they are, and we need those in leadership and elected positions to do something about it. Laredo has a thirty percent poverty rate. The percentage of people lacking health insurance is three times the national average. These kinds of statistics are all too common in Latino communities in the United States. We need our laws and systems to acknowledge and remedy the discriminatory differences that exist in our communities so that everyone can have the same opportunities.

Legacy of land ownership is an essential theme in *Judgment Reversed*. As I returned home to our family's ranch to care for Dad before his death, I thought a lot about the land and what we would eventually do with it. Did my brothers and I have the means to keep it, and what would it mean if we chose not to keep it?

Both Mom and Dad came from landowning families, and they raised us to believe that owning land was essential. It seemed to make sense, deep down, but I was never really told a reason why. Thinking practically, I wondered whether the time and expense of maintaining and keeping the ranch would be possible or even worth it for me. The corona-virus pandemic changed my mind.

As the pandemic tore across the country in March 2020 and cities issued stay-at-home orders, people picked grocery stores clean of toilet paper and meat. Panic became a familiar feeling. What would happen to the food system if all workers had to stay at home? Would it be safe to eat food from the store if someone else had touched it in order to package it? Living on the ranch, I drew relief from knowing that I could hunt for and grow my food. I went on walks through the monte. I learned the names of plants surrounding me and their uses. I was comforted when I learned that I could find soap and medicine in the roots, leaves, and blossoms around me.

Land makes life possible. Without it, we cannot eat. Land ownership offers opportunity, freedom, a safety-net. Hispanic landowners in the U.S. are few and own less than two percent of all U.S. farmland. The reality for most Latino communities in the U.S. is that ideals like opportunity, freedom, and safety-nets are all too scarce. Achieving these ideals in Latino communities—and everywhere—demands a better judicial system, one that is impartial. One that Reynaldo dreams of in *Judgment Reversed*.

Virginia E. Palacios
Encinal, Texas
May 2020